AN END OF SUMMER

It's the start of summer, an exciting time for Jennifer Bruce. She's been chosen as an apprentice actress at the Kennebunkport Playhouse on the coast of Maine, and has a full summer to indulge her love of acting. But Jennifer finds herself playing the female romantic lead in private to two very different males: Buddy Phillips, a fellow student actor, and Tim Moore, the company's leading man, handsome, and seventeen years her senior . . .

W. E. D. ROSS

AN END
OF SUMMER

Complete and Unabridged

LINFORD
Leicester

First published in Great Britain in 1974 by
Robert Hale Limited
London

First Linford Edition
published 2008
by arrangement with
Robert Hale Limited
London

British Library CIP Data

Ross, W. E. D. (William Edward Daniel), *1912 –*
An end of summer.—Large print ed.—
Linford romance library
1. Love stories
2. Large type books
I. Title
823.9'14 [F]

ISBN 978–1–84782–340–3

Published by
F. A. Thorpe (Publishing)
Anstey, Leicestershire

Set by Words & Graphics Ltd.
Anstey, Leicestershire
Printed and bound in Great Britain by
T. J. International Ltd., Padstow, Cornwall

This book is printed on acid-free paper

To Frank Small, proprietor of the Shawmut Inn, mentioned in this story. An actual inn redolent of Maine atmosphere and situated on the Ocean at Kennebunkport. And to the memory of Bob Currier's famed Kennebunkport Playhouse, sadly now in ashes.

1

The drive from the exit of the Maine Turnpike at Kennebunk down to the town of Kennebunkport took only about ten minutes, but for twenty-one-year-old, blonde, and petitely attractive Jennifer Bruce it was a journey from the world of grim reality to a kind of magic countryside. The moment she crossed the wooden bridge leading into the centre of the village she was thrilled by the charm of its weathered buildings leaning close together with their rustic signs advertising everything from paperback bookshops to tiny second-floor coffee houses.

Across the river to the left there was the white spire of the Unitarian Church, which she'd so often seen in paintings of the town, and ahead there was the modern brick pharmacy and the ancient buildings across from it which housed an art gallery. Attached to the building were a number of signs pointing in several directions, the signs were hand-painted and lettered and indicated the Shawmut Inn, the Colony Hotel and the Kennebunkport Playhouse among other things.

The Kennebunkport Playhouse! That was the sign which meant the most to her. For she was on her way to join the apprentice group at the famous Maine playhouse. She carefully selected the street ahead and drove up the hill to the intersection, where a fine old white-columned house gave the impression of the street coming to a dead end. But this was not the case. She saw another sign for the playhouse and this one pointed left. She swung her tiny yellow sub-compact car to the left and kept on that street for several minutes until she came to the third sign, which directed her to the right and brought her in sight of the large red barn playhouse, its sizeable parking lot and, in the field behind it, the several outbuildings where the actors, staff and apprentices lived.

She thrilled to the sight of the long barn theatre with its verandas in front and to the sides. There were steps leading to the box office and a few people were standing in line now, buying tickets for some future performance as it was only mid-June and the playhouse did not open until the week of July Fourth, when all the Maine resort towns came fully alive. She drove past the cars of the ticket buyers and headed towards a three-storey yellow building which had been described to her in a letter from the theatre's owner. This was where the majority of the apprentices lived and where she would be staying for the next eleven weeks!

Eleven weeks in the company of a professional theatre group. Her happy young heart beat more wildly at the prospect of it. It was the fulfilment of her most desired wish at this moment. Jennifer had grown up in Danvers, just outside Boston, and when she'd finished high school she'd persuaded her accountant father to let her attend Emerson College and study dramatics. Both her father and mother had been dubious about the venture, but she'd won them over to it.

Three years had passed since she'd entered Emerson, and in that time she'd learned a lot about being an actress. It had not changed her wanting to devote her life to theatre. She was now equipped with a degree to teach dramatics at the high school level and there was a job waiting for her in her home town at the beginning of the school season. In the meanwhile she'd had this opportunity to be an apprentice at Kennebunkport. There would be no money for her beyond her room and board, but she would gain a great deal of experience and, if she were lucky, she might get some small parts in the weekly professional productions mounted there. That was the important thing. A lucky break in such a part could lead to other roles in professional companies. Plays were sometimes tried out in summer theatres and seen by the producers planning to take them to Broadway. If such a producer saw a talent which fitted a particular role well, the actor or actress could often find themselves with a Broadway contract.

It was a dream! But one she couldn't give up. She was willing to compromise and teach drama in the school system for a few years. But before she settled down to any lasting way of life she wanted her chance at being a regular actress in the theatre, television or the movies. Her father and mother were conservative and she was their only daughter. It had been a wrench for them to allow her to live in that Bohemian Commonwealth Avenue apartment with three other girl students attending Emerson. And they would likely have objected to this summer in Kennebunkport had they not been familiar with the quaint town from spending summers there. Her father had attended college with the owner of the Shawmut Inn and the family often spent part of their holidays in the charming hotel situated directly on the ocean.

As she brought her car up before the entrance of the big yellow house she saw that there were an assortment of battered small cars and several motorcycles in the parking lot beside it. At least most of the young people working at the theatre would have their own means of transportation. She'd been duly warned by her parents not to crowd her car or engage in any reckless driving. They had also let her know they planned to spend some weekends at the Shawmut Inn so they could attend the plays at the playhouse and also keep an eye on her.

She didn't mind. The main thing was that she had been given a job as an apprentice and had a summer of opportunity before her. Her tanned, oval face wore a bright look of expectation as she got out of the car and made her way to the screen door of the apprentices' boarding house. She was wearing white slacks and a blue and white striped sleeveless pullover. The drive down the turnpike from Danvers had been a warm one and she now enjoyed the cool, salt-tanged air of this village by the sea.

She knocked on the door and waited on the steps. After a moment a mammoth woman in a print dress came to study her through the screen door. The woman had grey hair and a round, matronly face.

'Yes?' she said, betraying her Maine origin even in this single word, which came out with a slight nasal drawl.

'My name is Jennifer Bruce,' she said. 'I'm here as one of the apprentice company. I was told by Roger Deering I would be living here.'

'That's right,' the big woman said without enthusiam. 'You are the last to arrive. We've got a dozen of you here, so you'll have to take the accommodation that's left.'

'I'm not the fussy type,' she said.

'That's a blessing,' the big woman

said. 'Wouldn't do to be one here. You can park your car in the lot and bring in your bags. I'll show you to your room.'

'Thank you,' she said. The entire conversation had been conducted through the screen door. She went back to the tiny yellow car and backed it into an empty space in the parking lot. Then she took her two bags out of the back seat. The trunk had not been large enough to hold them.

With a sigh she picked up the bags and started across to the front door of the yellow house. The bags were heavy and tugged at her arms. As she neared the door a fat youth with a mop of unruly black hair appeared. He was also on his way to the house. He had a rather solemn face with heavy-lidded brown eyes. His serious face was in contradiction to his stout figure.

He at once came up to her and in a pleasant voice asked, 'Let me carry your bags for you. They look heavy.'

She smiled. 'They are heavy! But

that's no reason why I should burden you with them.'

He chuckled. 'Don't take that women's lib business too seriously. Let me offer a little old-fashioned male chivalry if I want to.'

'Well,' she said, her eyes twinkling, 'since you put it that way.' And she set down the bags.

He reached for them. 'Are you going to be an apprentice?'

'Yes.'

'So am I,' he said. 'My name is Randy Scott. I was a whiz in high school dramatics and last month I lost my job in a service station in my home town. So I decided I'd try being an actor.'

'This could be a good place to start,' she said.

'I've got to make good this summer,' the stout young man said seriously. 'Where are you from?'

'Danvers. I've studied at Emerson.'

'I've heard of it,' he said as he opened the screen door. 'I'm from a little town in Vermont.'

'I like Vermont,' she told him as she followed him inside.

Randy set her bags down on the linoleum-covered floor of the hallway. He showed a good-humoured smile on his fat face as he said, 'I come from a little town named Wilmington.'

'I've driven through there with my folks,' she remembered. 'It has a general store at the crossroads with a big sign.'

'That's right,' he said, delighted to meet anyone who knew something about his home town. 'That's Izacks's Store!'

She nodded. 'That's the name. It's a pretty little town.'

'Lots of mountains,' he said. 'I like it here. I've always liked the ocean.'

'Well, this is an ocean resort,' she said.

'This is not exactly the Grand Hotel,' he warned her. 'And on top of that it's pretty crowded.'

'I expected that.'

'Pretty good bunch, though.'

'That's the main thing,' she said.

'We're pretty busy now.'

'What are you doing?'

'I want to act,' he said. 'Right now I'm painting scenery.'

She laughed. 'Well, you're getting close.'

'Not close enough,' he said. 'I play a little guitar.'

'That can be fun.'

'Just for myself,' he said. 'Is Mrs Thatcher expecting you?'

'Yes. I talked with her a few minutes ago.'

He glanced down the hall. 'She ought to be here now. It's getting near dinner time. But then, she works in the kitchen, too. She's a widow and she makes her living running this place in summer. She also runs a snack lunch bar and regular bar for folks after the theatre. It's in the house on the road by the theatre itself.'

Jennifer was impressed. 'She must keep busy.'

The fat youth stood at the bottom of the stairway with her bags and called out, 'Mrs Thatcher!'

The big, matronly woman in the print dress appeared in the shadowed hallway and said, 'Oh, yes. She's to go all the way up to the third floor. Room ten.'

Randy Scott nodded glumly. 'I might have known it would be the top floor.' And he told Jennifer, 'Follow me.'

She was apologetic about the bags. 'Let me take one of them,' she suggested.

'No. I can manage easier with the two,' he assured her as he started up the narrow flight of stairs.

Jennifer followed him and noted that he was puffing heavily as they started up the second flight. She knew with his weight the bags must be quite a strain and she felt embarrassed. At last they reached the attic level of the house. She saw that the ceiling was cut in at spots where the outside walls slanted slightly inward.

The fat youth gasped, 'Ten is down to the right!'

'You're exhausted!' she sympathised.

'Good for me,' he said.

They came to an open door at the end of the hall and she saw that it was a big room with three single beds in it. A tall, slim brunette in a red bikini had come to the door to greet them. She had a sulky sort of olive-skinned beauty which exuded sex-appeal. The type bound to be popular with the boys!

'Hi, Two-Ton!' was her greeting. 'Are you moving in with us? Great!'

The fat Randy Scott went by her and planked the bags down heavily. He then produced a handkerchief from the rear pocket of his faded blue jeans and mopped his brow. 'This is your new room-mate,' he said.

'No kidding?' the svelte, red-bikinied one said, staring at Jennifer with undisguised curiosity. 'You look like the wholesome, idealistic type!'

Jennifer smiled at the other girl. 'I'm strong for causes! But don't ask me to go on any hunger strikes, it would ruin my figure.'

The fat Randy Scott gave her a warm grin. 'Guess you can take care of yourself. This is Sybil March, she's a kind of phoney. And that's Helen Murray stretched out on the bed. She's the best actress in the whole apprentice group.'

'Thank you, Two-Ton!' a cheery voice came from the bed which was partly hidden by the room's open door. At the same time a rather wistful, comic sort of face topped by a head of curly auburn hair peered beyond the door. It was not an ugly face, but certainly not a pretty one.

'See you all later,' the fat youth said, and waddled out.

'I do believe you're shy, Two-Ton!' the slender girl in the red bikini called after him as she stood there with a hand on her shapely thigh.

The plain, auburn-haired girl sat up on her bed and studied Jennifer. The girl had on a cheap pair of blue shorts and a white halter top. Her skin was of the very milky-white type of most redheads and she had some bad sunburn on her bare arms and shoulders.

She said, 'What's your name?'

'Jennifer Bruce,' she told the girl, whom she instantly decided she would like better than the brunette, Sybil.

'Now that's a name for a leading lady if I ever heard one,' Helen marvelled. 'Is it your own?'

'Yes.'

'You're lucky!' Helen said. 'My name happens to be Meritzky! How would you like a tag like that? So my stage name is Helen Murray.'

Sybil came undulating up to join the conversation. With a bored look on her sulky-pretty face she said, 'Have you had any experience?'

Jennifer said, 'I've graduated from Emerson College of Drama. I have my teaching licence and a job in high school for the fall. I've also done a lot of school dramatics.'

'Teaching!' the brunette drawled, as if it were a disgusting word. 'High school dramatics! I'd hardly call that experience!'

'Don't be so uppity!' Helen Murray told the bikini beauty from the bed. 'What have you done that is so great?'

Sybil raised a pert chin. 'I'm a graduate of the American Academy of Dramatic Art and I live and work in New York. Just now I'm doing modelling.'

Helen jumped up with a wryly amused look on her plain face. 'Modelling! I love that!' She turned to Jennifer and said, 'I'll tell you the kind of modelling she's done. She's worked as a demonstrator in department stores. You know what I mean! One week she's Miss Camera taking snapshots of the customers. The next she's in the basement demonstrating some trick potato-peeler!'

'Well, it takes dramatic talent just the same!' Sybil said petulantly. 'And I didn't have to change my name.'

'I would change it if I took jobs like that,' Helen Murray said with comic bleakness.

'What have you done?' Jennifer asked the red-head.

'I left college to study in London for a year at the Royal Academy,' Helen said. 'Now I specialise in British accents. I've done a few television commercials and I've worked in very small semi-professional stage groups in New York.'

Sybil smiled nastily. 'They play in basements so isolated and so far underground no one can find them.'

'All right, potato-peeler!' Helen said. 'We never have accepted you as the company dramatic critic.'

Jennifer was amused by the clash between the two girls. They were completely different types, but she felt she could get along with them.

She said, 'I hope I won't be crowding you.'

'Don't worry about that,' the redhead said. 'All the rooms are filled. Most of them have at least three in them. Part of the staff stay here along with the apprentices. The bathroom for this floor is down at the other end of the hall and you'd better be in line early in the morning as Miss Sybil hogs it for a full thirty minutes when she gets in there.'

The brunette Sybil said, 'I'm used to a bath of my own!'

'And servants,' Helen mocked her. 'And a dressing-room just for your clothes alone!'

'Well, my parents have given me those things,' Sybil said with anger. 'Being here is a sacrifice for my art!'

Helen grimaced and spread her hands for Jennifer's benefit. 'You may as well get used to rooming with Helen Hayes!' she said wryly.

Sybil showed an unexpected friendly side to her nature as she enquired of Jennifer, 'May I help you unpack? You can have the bed by the window if you like.'

'Thanks,' she said. 'I think I can manage alone. But I should get at it. It will soon be dinner time.'

'That's right,' Helen agreed, sitting on her bed again. 'And we have a rehearsal at seven.'

'I wondered if you'd started,' she said

as she lifted one of the bags on to the bed by the window and began to unpack. 'What is the first play?'

Helen said, 'It's 'No Sex Please — We're British'. A really funny comedy. Roger Deering is directing it and the British television interviewer Donald Winter is the guest star. Of course, the regular leading man of the company, Tim Moore, plays an important part. He's starring in the next production, which is Noel Coward's 'Blithe Spirit'. He's been leading man of the company for years!'

Sybil chimed in, 'And both Helen and I have parts in the play.'

'Good!' Jennifer said sincerely as she went to the small closet and pushed aside the clothing there to hang up some of her dresses.

'Small parts,' Helen explained. 'I have a few lines and Sybil mainly shows off her figure. But they'll be fun doing.'

Sybil pounced on a yellow jump suit which Jennifer produced from the second bag which she'd now opened. 'I adore this! And we're about the same size,' the bikini-clad girl said. 'Would you let me wear it some time?'

Jennifer wasn't sure she liked the idea, but she didn't want to make a fuss about it so soon after arriving. She said, 'I guess so, if it really does fit you. I'm shorter than you.'

'Not much!' Sybil said, holding the smart jump suit up against her and going to the room's single full-length mirror to study herself in it.

Helen made a weary gesture. 'Now you know why she's being so helpful. She takes an interest in clothes. Other people's!'

Jennifer hurried with her unpacking and then went down to the old-fashioned bathroom which served the entire floor and freshened up. By the time she returned Sybil Marsh had changed into dark slacks and a white blouse. Helen was standing waiting by the door.

The red-haired girl said, 'We'll escort you down to dinner. You may as well sit at our table. I can get an extra chair put there.'

'It's the best table in the dining-room,' Sybil explained. 'We're by a big window with a screen in it and when the weather is warm the dining-room can get hot.'

'And we've boys at our table,' Helen told her with a wink. 'Your friend Two-Ton for one, and a lanky boy from Boston called Peter Bayfield, and Buddy Phillips.'

'Buddy is a dreamboat!' Sybil said rapturously as the three of them started down the stairs.

'Oh?' Jennifer said.

Helen, a step ahead of her, said in a low voice, 'He's the son of a wealthy hotel-owner. They have a string of the new dinner-theatres, where you buy dinner and see a play afterwards in the same room free. He's here to study production and stage management. He's not interested in acting, though he's good looking enough to be an actor.'

'But he's too young for anyone to be

seriously interested in him,' Sybil drawled in her superior way.

'I've seen you trying to get his attention often enough,' Helen told her. 'He's around our own age, twenty-one or two.'

'I prefer older men,' Sybil said.

'I'll take anything male that comes along,' Helen told her in her comic fashion.

They reached the ground floor and went to the big dining-room with its red-checkered tablecloths and round tables. Helen led her to the table by the window. Two-Ton was already seated there and when he saw the three girls approaching he stood up. By his side another young man had risen to a standing position. He was tall, sandy-haired and had a pleasant, thin face with a nice smile.

This young man's eyes met Jennifer's in a friendly glance as he said, 'I'll get another chair!' And he moved away to look after this.

Jennifer had no doubt that this was

the popular Buddy Phillips who was causing many a heart throb among the girls of the company. She felt it was easy to understand why.

2

Buddy Phillips returned with her chair for her and set it between Randy's chair and his own. He smiled and said, 'I'll have the waitress set a place for you.'

'Thank you,' she said, sitting down. Sybil and Helen had already taken their places at the table.

Buddy said, 'You're the new girl.'

'Yes,' she said. 'I'm Jennifer Bruce.' And she went on to tell him something of her background.

'You should enjoy it here,' the pleasant young man said. 'And you ought to get some good experience as well. Roger Deering used to act with some of the biggest stars and he is an excellent director.'

'I've heard about him,' she agreed.

Buddy nodded towards the other tables. 'We have a wide range of types among the apprentices, as you can see.'

She studied the other tables and saw that some of the boys and girls were younger than their group. She said, 'Some of them seem quite young.'

'Directly out of high school,' he said. 'They mostly do errands and usher and that sort of thing. Our table is the older age group. Of course, there are the technical staff of stagehands, electricians, prop men and scenic artists at the other tables.'

She saw this group of more mature adults and noticed that they were paying no attention to the other tables. They had their own interests and conversation. They were also paid professionals and the superiors of the unpaid apprentices living in the boarding house.

She said, 'I can see there is a class distinction even here. We are sort of among the untouchables.'

He laughed. 'It's not quite that bad. The staff are very pleasant with the apprentices. And so, for the most part, are the professional company.'

'Where do they live?'

'In the house on the other side of the playhouse,' he said. 'All except Roger Deering and the stars. He sends the visiting players to a nice little inn along the River Road called the Homestead. And he lives in the cottage just beyond this.'

She said, 'You're working with the staff?'

'Yes.' And he repeated the information Helen had already given her. He was only interested in gaining a knowledge of production so he could take over the management of the half-dozen dinner-theatres in his father's hotels.

The girl serving them set her place and brought the several courses of the good plain food which was featured in the boarding house. The entrée on this occasion was broiled haddock, and she thought it excellent.

From across the table Helen smiled knowingly and said, 'Well, I see you two didn't need any introductions.'

'We've already taken care of that,'

Buddy Phillips assured her.

Sybil's sulky face showed a faint smile and she said, 'Jennifer wants to act, so we're all going to be faced with some extra competition.'

Randy's fat face showed a grin as he told her, 'She's not going to be any competition for you in that bikini, honey child!'

Sybil pouted. 'I can do more than wear a bikini, Two-Ton!'

The plain Helen told her, 'Two-Ton is right! You do that best!'

Buddy Phillips, by way of placating the brunette girl, told Jennifer, 'Helen and Sybil are in the first show and they're great.'

'The parts are small,' Helen said, sipping her coffee.

'Still, you're right for them, and that's the main thing,' he said.

'The trouble is that the play was seen on Broadway last year, so we'll have no producers or scouts here to look at it,' Sybil lamented.

Jennifer turned to Buddy again and

said, 'I understand there is a rehearsal at seven. I want to see Roger Deering and let him know I'm here. Where would I be likely to find him?'

'In the theatre,' the sandy-haired young man said. 'He is having the rehearsal on stage as we open next Monday. He generally sits about mid-way down the theatre on the aisle.'

'I'll remember that.'

'He's generally friendly,' Buddy said. 'Now and then he gets annoyed. At those times it's best to keep out of his way.'

They finished dinner and then went outside for ten minutes or so. It was a warm, June evening and the small flower garden in front of the yellow house was in full bloom. After a little everyone began to drift over to the big red barn playhouse. Jennifer felt a slight uneasiness, not sure how the well-known director would receive her.

She entered the theatre by a side door which led to the outside refreshment stand. As soon as she left the sunlight of the early evening and stepped into the near darkness of the playhouse she experienced the feeling of excitement which theatres invariably gave her. She stood just inside the door for a moment to get her bearings.

The stage to her left was already lighted, though there were no actors in view yet. Furniture was in place for the rehearsal and the set was up. It was a living-room scene with a partition at the rear partially concealing a kitchen. A stagehand and Buddy Phillips were rearranging a divan which was one of the pieces on the set.

Down in the main body of the theatre she saw someone seated on the aisle. Since she'd been told this was where she'd find the director and producer, Roger Deering, she rather timidly made her way down the middle aisle to the seated man.

'Good evening,' she said.

'Good evening,' he replied pleasantly. He was a handsome man, probably in his forties, but well preserved. He had classic, even features and no matter where anyone might see him they would at once think of him as an actor.

'I wanted to see you before the rehearsal began,' Jennifer faltered.

'Oh?'

'I arrived this afternoon. My name is Jennifer Bruce.'

The man stood up, he was a head taller than she. He said, 'I'm glad to know you, Jennifer.'

'I hope I'll work out all right for you, Mr Deering.'

The handsome man smiled. 'I'm sure you'll be an asset to the playhouse. However, there is just one catch. I'm not Roger Deering.'

She at once felt ridiculous. 'I'm terribly sorry,' she said.

'No need to be,' he said at once. 'I imagine you were told you'd find Roger here. I happen to be waiting for him and I sat where he usually sits. So it's not your fault at all.'

'Thank you,' she said. 'You make me feel less silly.'

'It was a natural mistake,' he told her. 'My name is Tim Moore.'

Her eyebrows raised. 'Of course! You're the leading man of the company!'

He smiled modestly. 'From time to time. What have you done in the theatre before coming here?'

She told him and he listened with friendly interest. She ended by asking him, 'How long have you been leading man at the Kennebunkport Playhouse?'

'I'm afraid answering that means giving my age away,' he told her. 'I had my first season here ten years ago. And the next year I became leading man.'

'That's a wonderful record!' she enthused.

'It has been great fun,' he agreed. 'In the regular season I've usually had a Broadway show or two. They sometimes don't run too long. And I've done some soap-opera television work and a few small movie parts.'

'You should be very proud of your career,' she said.

'It's a modest one,' he assured her.

At that moment another man came slowly up the aisle to join them. He was shorter than Tim Moore and inclined to stoutness. He also had the rather dashing look of an actor, though he was not as good looking as the leading man and his hair was greying.

Tim at once said, 'Roger, I'd like you to meet Jennifer Bruce. She's an apprentice and she arrived this afternoon.'

'Ah, yes,' Roger Deering said. 'I remember our correspondence. Your father is a friend of the Shawmut Inn owner, Fred Short.'

She nodded. 'He and my father were college classmates.'

'Fred mentioned that,' Roger Deering said. He had a weary air about him. 'You know that Fred is one of the playhouse shareholders?'

'No, I didn't,' she said.

'He has a large share in our project,' Roger Deering said. 'Better than that, he takes an active interest in it. I hope you will be happy with us, Miss Bruce.'

'I'm sure I will be.'

The theatre director eyed her appraisingly. 'I like your appearance. Before the summer is out we'll discover if you have any ability to back it up.'

She blushed. 'I hope so.'

Roger Deering said, 'Just now we need a prompt girl and I see no reason why you shouldn't take over. See Ken Chadwick, the stage manager, and he'll turn the prompt book over to you. You'll sit in the wings and give the actors any lines they need. Some of the cast still haven't gotten their parts memorised perfectly.'

'Thank you,' she said, pleased to so soon be given a task.

'Fine,' the director said in his weary fashion, dismissing her by turning away from her.

Tim Moore flashed her an encouraging smile. 'I'm one of those who'll need your help, Jennifer. Best of luck!'

'Thank you,' she said again. As she walked away from the two men she heard them enter into an earnest discussion about the casting of the following week's play. She remembered that it was to be 'Blithe Spirit' and Tim was playing the lead. No doubt he was concerned that it should be cast just right.

There was no direct entrance to the stage from the theatre auditorium so she had to go out by the side door again and mount a flight of steps which led to the stage door. Inside she passed a long area of cubicles which were the dressing-rooms of the company. Their doors were mostly closed, but she could hear voices from inside some of them as the walls forming the cubicles did not go all the way to the high roof of the backstage section of the playhouse.

She went on to the lighting board, which was to the right of the stage proper. There she found the electrician, Buddy Phillips, Randy Scott and a tall, thin man with a bald head and small black moustache. She at once guessed he must be the stage manager as he had a certain air of authority.

'Mr Chadwick?' she asked in a small voice.

'I'm Ken Chadwick,' he said. 'What do you want?'

'I'm told to hold the script,' she said. 'Mr Deering said you'd give me a copy.'

'Did he?' the bald man said.

'Yes.' She saw that Buddy and Randy were smiling and so was the electrician.

'Let me tell you, young lady, I don't envy you your job,' Ken Chadwick said. 'Our director gets very short-tempered when actors forget lines at this late date in rehearsals and some of our people aren't set in their lines yet.'

'Especially Donald Winter!' Buddy Phillips exclaimed. 'He blew up a half-dozen times last night.'

Randy Scott nodded. 'And that put Tim Moore off!'

'I know all about it,' the lanky stage manager said dismally. 'You don't need to refresh my memory.' He went over to a table and picked up a blue bound copy of the bulky script. Handing it to her, he said, 'It's all yours, my girl.'

'Thanks,' she said, taking it and going over to a nearby chair to sit down and familiarise herself with it.

She'd only been there a few minutes when Buddy Phillips came and stood by her. He said, 'Watch your step! I don't want you to be let go the first night you're here. Try and get the lines out quickly if they seem to need them and don't let Roger Deering rattle you.'

'I'll try not to,' she said with a nervous smile.

'We had one of the really young apprentices holding the book last night,' Buddy went on. 'She left in hysterics before the end of the second act. But tonight shouldn't be so hard. Most of them will have done some more studying of their roles.'

'I hope so,' she said. And after he left her to attend to some task, she renewed her study of the script.

Gradually backstage became a hive of activity. Actors began to appear and the star, Donald Winter, came to stand in the wings and chat nervously with Tim

Moore. He seemed a very tense little man with a precise British accent which was exactly right for the play.

From the auditorium Roger Deering called, 'Let's get going!' He didn't sound too patient.

Jennifer stood up and moved across to the wings at a spot where she could see the actors on the stage and yet not be seen by the people in the body of the theatre. Ken Chadwick had the curtain lowered and then lifted it on the action of the play. Tim Moore, as a worried young husband, had the first scene with an attractive golden-haired girl, playing his wife. Their scene went well. It was followed by the entrance of Donald Winter as an eccentric bank employee.

Jennifer made herself keep her eyes on the prompt book as she followed the show, line by line. Donald Winter was fine in the role, combining just the right amount of comic dignity with a frantic, farcical nervousness. She found herself enjoying the funny play and actually laughing a little to herself.

Then it happened! At an especially fast-moving moment in the first act Donald Winter stuttered and couldn't think of his next line. She at once called out the line to him and he went on with the scene. But this was not to be the end of it. Within two or three minutes he paused for a line again. Before she could give him the line there was a cry of protest from the dark body of the playhouse.

'No! No! No!' Roger Deering shouted. 'That will never do. Donald, you are ruining the play!'

The frosty-manner Britisher stared down at the director from the stage. 'Sorry, old chap,' he said. 'I'll get those few lines set before tomorrow.'

'You told me that yesterday!' Roger Deering chided him.

'I've been working at it,' Donald Winter said, as the other actors stood by silently. 'I have a good idea of what to say. All I need is a key word to cue me. The young lady with the prompt book is a little slow coming in with my line and she reads me the whole line instead of just tossing me a couple of key words.'

From the auditorium there came a weary shout. 'You, up there! Jennifer, what's your name! Come out where I can see you!'

Feeling thoroughly miserable, she advanced out on the stage with the prompt book in her hand. 'Yes?' she said, staring down into the yawning darkness of the empty seats.

Below in the theatre Roger Deering cried, 'I know you are an amateur, young woman. But try and be more alert. We don't want to hear you reading the lines. We want you to get the gist of the line to Mr Winter quickly so he can carry on without a noticeable break.'

'Yes, sir,' she said meekly.

'Very well, let us begin again,' the director said.

The scene was replayed and everything went well until near the end of the act. Then Donald Winter said a wrong line and Tim Moore came back with a wrong one and they both could go no further. Silence filled the stage as they broke the action, this was followed by another explosion of anger from Roger Deering in the theatre.

This was the pattern for the evening. Feeling thoroughly dejected, Jennifer attempted to get the prompt lines out more quickly and she did succeed in this. After she'd gained the knack of it the task wasn't so awful. But Roger Deering continued in a bad humour and several times stopped the show again.

At last the rehearsal ended and she went back into the wings with the prompt book, feeling thoroughly let down. Ken Chadwick was standing there talking to the fat Randy Scott.

The lanky stage manager told her, 'You did well for a first time.'

'That's so,' Randy said with a serious expression on his round face.

'At least you didn't run off in hysterics,' the stage manager congratulated her.

'Not that I didn't want to,' she said.

'You'll be in better shape tomorrow night,' Ken Chadwick said. 'And so I hope will Donald Winter. He has to know his lines some time soon.'

The stout youth said, 'I've heard he's very bad at study.'

'You can tell that by watching him forget lines night after night,' the tall Ken Chadwick said with disgust. 'It wasn't Tim Moore's fault that he forgot his lines, it was trying to work with Winter. He threw him completely off the track.'

'That is true,' she agreed.

Randy smiled at her. 'Anyway, it looks as if you've got the prompt job sewed up.'

'I'm afraid so,' she agreed ruefully. And she asked the lanky stage manager, 'May I take the book to my room with me? I'd like to become more familiar with the play.'

'By all means,' Ken said. 'I approve of the idea.'

Randy warned her, 'With Helen and

Sybil in the same room, you won't get much studying in.'

'I'm pretty good at concentrating,' she said. 'I think I'll manage.'

Just then Buddy Phillips came by. He stopped to tell her, 'Don't worry about what Roger said. I think you were great.'

'I'm going to improve. I'm finding out how it's done.'

'Bound to take a little time,' the pleasant young man agreed. 'How did you like Helen and Sybil?'

She laughed. 'They were just right!'

'I think so,' Buddy said. 'If I were a casting director I'd put them in those parts. I guess I'll be handling that job for my father's shows pretty soon.'

'That will be a lot of responsibility.'

'I know. It's why I'm here. I'm trying to get the knack of things, just as you are.'

Randy gave the other young man a wink. 'You'd better find jobs for us all.'

Buddy laughed. 'I promise you'll get the first fat man role.'

The fat youth winced. 'All anyone sees in me is fat. Why don't they look closer and see the dramatic actor!'

Ken Chadwick told him, 'Because he's hiding behind the fat. Reduce or play fat man roles all your life!'

Randy shook his head dolefully. 'Guess I'll have to be content to work behind the scenes.'

Buddy said, 'Maybe we can stroll back to the house together. I've still got a few things to do here. I'll be back in a few minutes.'

Jennifer smiled. 'All right. I'll not be leaving right away.' She had found the serious Buddy very nice and felt she'd like to know him better. Certainly with his father's productions to give him a start, he ought to have a very good future in the theatre.

She was standing in the wings thinking about this when all at once the handsome Tim Moore came striding across the stage to greet her.

'You made me proud of you, Jennifer,' he said for a start.

'You're trying to make me feel good.'

'No. I mean it.'

'Roger Deering wasn't so enthusiastic,' she reminded him.

The leading man laughed. 'You must have heard that Roger is invariably difficult at rehearsals. It's one of his traits. A little hard on all of us, but the important thing is that he nearly always brings in a good show.'

'I'm sure he's brilliant.'

'He is. So don't be depressed.' He hesitated. 'I have an idea. Let me take you somewhere for a drink and to relax before you go to your boarding place.'

She was realising how much she admired the handsome actor. She said, 'I don't want to impose on you.'

'No imposition! I'd enjoy it,' he said in his friendly way.

'Very well,' she said.

'I've got my car parked outside,' he told her. They left the backstage together with her forgetting all about her promise to wait for Buddy Phillips.

3

The air was cool now, as most nights in Maine tend to be. She walked across the parking lot with the leading man until they came to a low-slung, dark, foreign sports car. He halted and unlocked the door on the passenger side for her.

'This is my Jag,' he said casually as he opened the door. 'It's not the latest vintage, but a great car. I came down here from New York in no time.'

'I like these style cars,' Jennifer told him. 'They are very foreign-agenty, if you know what I mean.'

'I think I do,' Tim said, closing the door. He went around and got behind the wheel of the car and started it. As they drove away from the playhouse she had a moment's glimpse of Buddy Phillips coming out on the platform by the stage door and looking around as if searching for her. She felt a brief flash of guiltiness and then assuaged her feelings by promising that she would explain it to the young man.

She hunched back in the car's bucket seat and gazed out at the river with its many power and sail boats tied at the various marinas as they passed. 'What a lot of boating is done here,' she said.

'A great many of them are visitors,' Tim explained from the wheel. 'They come here for a day or two, sometimes just for overnight. It gives the marinas extra business and the hotels and restaurants benefit as well. So does the theatre.'

'The business side is important,' she agreed.

'Most important,' he said. 'Roger tries to balance his choice of plays so that everyone will be satisfied. And that is not easy to do.'

'I'm sure of that,' she agreed. 'I'd say the present play ought to please nearly everybody.'

At the wheel Tim's handsome face

showed a reflective expression. He said, 'Don't be too sure. The Theatre Board is hard to satisfy. They're always looking over at Ogunquit with longing eyes. They have a package programme over there and its only a twenty minutes drive.'

'Package programme?' she asked.

'You know what I mean,' the leading man said. 'We bring our stars in and rehearse the play around them with our resident players. We sometimes have no stars, but the resident company does the play alone. Whereas theatres like Ogunquit have no resident company at all, and only a few apprentices. It actually is more of a booking agency than anything else.'

'I know,' she agreed. 'A play is rehearsed with a star and cast and sent around a circuit of theatres.'

'Ogunquit is the outlet in this area,' the actor said. 'It gives them big stars and eliminates the problems of local productions. On the other hand, producing the plays locally gives you a better selection to choose from and you can fit the package to your particular situation.'

'Which is best?'

'I prefer the way we do it here,' Tim Moore said. 'But the trend is the other way. Every year there are more package deals.'

'I see,' she said.

'Having several months' work in different plays here every year is good for me as an actor and it also gives me a sure amount of work on which to build my year's earnings.'

'I can understand that,' she agreed.

He slowly headed the car around a turn and then into an asphalt roadway which ran in a semi-circle before a large resort-type hotel. The huge white colonial building was well spotlighted and its lobby doors were open to reveal a pleasant, informal room with wood-panelled walls.

Tim swung the car into the first open parking space they found just beyond the hotel entrance. He said, 'This is The

Colony. It's a pleasant place to spend some time after the theatre.'

'And it's not all that far from the playhouse,' she said.

He got out and opened her door for her and they strolled to a ground-floor entrance with a sign, 'The Marine Room' over it.

He opened one of the French doors leading into a long, wide hallway and said, 'On the weekends they have music and dancing here. But early in the week it's very quiet.'

'It's certainly a large hotel,' she said, impressed as they went down the shadowed hallway to the lounge.

'Over a half-century old,' Tim said. They reached the lounge and a pleasant, dark young man led them to a table in an outer area whose glass walls gave a view of the ocean, the harbour and the adjoining Kennebunk Beach area. She sat watching the myriad of lights along the beach and the star-filled sky reflecting on the dark ocean.

'What a wonderful view!' she enthused.

'I've been here before with my parents when I was younger. But I think it had to be in the daytime so the view seemed different. It's very hazy in my mind.'

'You've been here before?' he said, across the table.

'When I was young, and then with my parents. We stayed at the Shawmut Inn. I rarely remember us leaving the hotel grounds during our stay. So I don't know all that much about the town.'

The handsome leading man smiled. 'At the Shawmut you wouldn't have to venture anywhere else for entertainment. They have everything.'

'Now I'm seeing the town from a different viewpoint,' she said. 'It's going to be interesting.'

A waiter came and they ordered, and then Tim began to draw her out about her experience. She told him about her school plays and then her years at Emerson College.

She sighed. 'I'm not anxious to go into teaching, but my parents consider it the practical thing to do. They're very practical folk!'

He was studying her with quiet amusement. 'Being practical isn't all that bad. If you don't carry it too far.'

'That's exactly the point,' she said. 'I have a fear that they do.'

'Then just guard against it,' he said. 'A year or two of teaching won't do you any harm. You may be able to pick up some summer professional jobs or even some television work in Boston since you won't be far from there.'

'And there are a few companies who do weekend productions,' she told him. 'That means a teacher like myself can work in them after her five days' teaching is done.'

He smiled. 'So there are lots of possibilities.'

'None like the real theatre,' she said wistfully. 'You were in a Broadway play last year, I've heard.'

'That's right. I was in a comedy called, 'Come Back Tomorrow'. We're going to do it here in a few weeks. It wasn't any big hit, I'm afraid.'

'Still, just to be in it!' She gave a great sigh.

Tim studied her with those twinkling eyes. 'We all feel that way at first. Then it becomes less exciting. You worry more about merely getting a job than being on Broadway. I've been in six Broadway shows.'

'Wonderful! Now I understand why Roger Deering advertises you as the New York Star!'

He laughed. 'I'd call that exaggeration.'

The waiter came with their order and they went on talking. Muzak played in the background, giving the dimly-lighted lounge some atmosphere, and there were a few other couples wandering in and out. At the bar a tall, good-looking man with curly dark hair sat, and with him on another of the stools was a smaller, slim man with horn-rimmed glasses.

Tim Moore said, 'You were just speaking about the Shawmut Inn.

There's the owner. He's sitting at the bar with Jim Fredericks, the manager of this hotel. No doubt discussing the season ahead.'

'That is Fred Short,' she said, staring in at the bar with the alert-looking man with the glasses was suddenly laughing as he and the manager of The Colony enjoyed some private joke.

'Yes,' Tim said. 'He's often at the theatre.'

'Really? He was a class-mate of my father's during their college days. I'm supposed to look him up.'

Tim said, 'Why don't you go and speak to him now?'

'Would it be all right?'

'Of course,' Tim said, standing. 'Go ahead. I'll wait here for you.'

'I won't be long,' she promised as she got up and went into the lounge proper. Approaching the bar, she halted beside the slim man with the glasses and in a timid voice, said, 'Mr Short?'

He turned to her rather casually. 'Yes?'

'Forgive me for interrupting,' she apologised, 'but you were pointed out to me and you're a friend of my father's.'

The face of the man on the stool brightened at once. 'You must be Jennifer Bruce!'

'Yes,' she said, pleased that he should know.

He slid off the stool and shook hands with her. 'Your Dad wrote me you were coming, but I didn't expect you so soon. You've grown up since I saw you last.'

'I know,' she said, embarrassed as she almost always was in the presence of her parents' friends.

'Are you all settled at the playhouse?' Fred Short asked.

'Yes.'

'Good. Roger Deering puts on excellent shows. I'm sure you will enjoy it.'

'I have no doubt about that,' she enthused. 'Tim Moore brought me here tonight. I believe it's a favourite place of his.'

Fred Short's eyebrows rose and the keen eyes behind his glasses were fixed on her with some curiosity showing in them. 'You're getting acquainted with the company fast. He has been leading man here ever since I took over the management of my hotel from my parents. That must be almost a decade ago.'

'He's a very good actor.'

'And a charming person,' Fred said with a thin smile. 'But won't you be shutting yourself off from the rest of the apprentices by associating with the leading members of the company?'

'I hadn't thought about that.'

'It's probaby not all that important,' Fred Short said. 'Let me know the first evening you are free. I want you to join me at the Shawmut for dinner.'

'Thank you,' she said. 'It will probably be Sunday.'

'That will do fine. I'm always there,' Fred Short said.

'My parents are coming down for some of the shows,' she said. 'They're planning to stay with you.'

'We'll find them a room,' Fred Short assured her. 'Or maybe Jim will,' he said, turning to include the younger man in their conversation. 'This is Jim Fredericks, who manages this place.'

'How do you do,' she said, noticing that the pleasant, curly-haired man was observing her with friendly interest.

'I don't get to any of the shows,' he said, 'the rush of the summer season being what it is. But I've heard great comments on the plays from my guests.'

Fred Short gave him a reproachful look. 'You should take the time to attend the theatre. I do.'

The man at the bar laughed. 'Let me know when you're in a play, Miss Bruce. I'll make an exception.'

Fred Short winked at Jennifer. 'Be sure you do that. I want to trap him in his own promise.'

'I will,' she said. 'I've enjoyed meeting you both.'

'Give my regards to Tim,' Fred Short

said as she left. And he also waved from the bar to Tim. The actor waved back as he rose to welcome her return to the table outside.

She sat down and said, 'I had a nice chat.'

'I thought you would,' Tim agreed. 'Fred Short has done a lot for the theatre. He's on the board.'

'So Roger Deering told me.' She felt so comfortable with Tim that she couldn't imagine there was anything wrong in her having this date with him.

The handsome leading man said, 'When we do 'Come Back Tomorrow' I want you to read for a part in it. There's a small part of a girl of divorced parents. She has a touching scene with her father. It's not a large role so we'll be casting it from the apprentices. I'd say it's just right for you. And almost every night the girl who played the part in New York got a hand on her exit and a big burst of applause when we took our curtain calls.'

Jennifer was at once excited. 'Do you

honestly think I'd suit the part?'

'Physically, yes. It will depend on your reading. I know Roger. He's scrupulously fair about such things and he's bound to give it to whoever offers the best reading.'

'I'll try hard.'

He said, 'I'll get a copy of the script before we do the show and coach you some of the way to shade the role. If it is played exactly right it's a winner.'

She sat back in her chair with a smile. 'I'm so happy just to be here. It's bound to be a wonderful summer.'

'I hope so,' he said sincerely. 'Of course, before you know it the season will be over. The end of summer comes and we rarely are ready for it.'

'An end of summer,' she mused. 'That has a sad ring to it.'

'I always find it a melancholy time,' the leading man agreed. 'It's the moment of breaking the friendships one has formed, saying goodbye to a familiar place and familiar people. I can't say that I enjoy it.'

'I don't want to see this summer ever end,' she said.

'I warn you, they all do,' Tim Moore said quietly.

She glanced in at the bar and saw that both Fred Short and the manager of the hotel had vanished. The place was almost empty now. She turned to Tim Moore again. 'This has been a wonderful evening for me. How kind of you to bring me here.'

He smiled. 'Selfish of me.'

'Selfish?' she repeated in surprise.

'Of course,' he said. 'I'm the one gaining all the benefits. I wasn't able to resist you this evening. Your youth, your love for the theatre and your attractive-ness were all too much for me. I had a strong desire to try and feel things through you. To get back a touch of my old enthusiasm once again. Being with you is a kind of renewal for me.'

She stared at him with baffled eyes. 'But I don't see you as old or even as world-weary.'

'Thanks,' Tim Moore said. 'But the

fact remains you could be my daughter. If I had a daughter I'd want her to be exactly like you.'

Jennifer's cheeks warmed. 'Thanks. But I don't think of you as a father. I look on you as a friend.'

'An older friend,' he amended her.

'No!' she protested. 'I think actors are ageless.'

'I'm sure we'd like to be,' Tim smiled sadly. 'I'm also afraid it is largely an illusion that we are. Still, I appreciate your tribute and I hope we can continue to be friends.'

'So do I,' she said fervently. 'I've enjoyed being with you so!'

'Probably you'd be having a lot more fun drinking beer in one of the taverns with the other apprentices. I hear they have a favourite hangout at the Dock.'

'No,' she said. 'I love this kind of evening. The boys in the company seem very nice, especially Buddy Phillips, but then, they are so young!'

'Don't scorn youth,' the actor warned her. 'Remember what Shakespeare tells us in 'Twelfth Night'? 'Then come kiss me, Sweet-and-Twenty, Youth's a stuff will not endure.' And how right that is!'

'Right now I'm impatient to be older,' she said.

'A passing phase,' was his comment. He signalled the waiter for the check. 'I'd better get you back to the boarding house or I'll be giving you a bad name the first night you're here.'

She laughed. 'That will only make me more interesting!'

Tim paid the waiter and they left the hotel lounge. Back in the car he drove slowly along the street fronting the river. He told her, 'The police keep a sharp traffic check here. It doesn't do to speed. And, anyway, I want to drag the evening out as long as possible.'

Jennifer gave him a tender glance in the semi-darkness and intimacy of the car's front seat. She said, 'It's strange, I feel the same way.'

'There will be more evenings for us,' he promised. 'There must be.'

'Yes!' she agreed emphatically. 'There

are so many things I want to hear about you. About what you've done in the theatre and what your life has been like.'

'That will take several evenings,' he assured her.

'Are you married?'

'No.'

There was something about the way he said it which made her go on and ask, 'Have you been?'

He nodded. 'I was married when I was around your age.'

'But it didn't last?'

'No.'

'Why?'

He kept his eyes on the road, his handsome profile grave as he spoke. 'It was doomed from the start. We were exactly the same age, so I was too young for her. I wanted to work in the theatre and she wanted me to take a clerking job in her father's shoe store.'

'Shoe store!' she said incredulously.

'It wasn't such a bad offer,' he quickly added. 'Her father owns a chain now and the fellow who married her after we were divorced is now the manager of all those stores.'

'But you didn't want that!'

'No,' he said wryly. 'I didn't want that. I had to be an actor. And so I became one.'

'I think that's marvellous,' she said impulsively. 'I'd have hated you if you'd remained married to that girl just to be the manager of a shoe store chain!'

'There was no chance of that,' he said, swinging the car into a narrow side street as they continued to head for the playhouse. 'I realised we didn't love each other. Didn't even like each other, really! And that's even worse.'

'So there could be no understanding.'

'None at all. We fought bitterly all the time we were married,' Tim said.

'Were there any children?'

'None,' he said. 'She has some now by her second husband. They came backstage to see me one night after a performance of a Broadway show I was in. It's funny but I think we were more pleased to see each other and happier together in those few minutes than we ever were in all our married life.'

'Because then you met as friends,' she suggested.

He gave her a glance. 'That's perceptive,' he said. 'We have been able to be friends but we couldn't manage as husband and wife.'

'Do you ever get lonely, being on your own?'

He shrugged. 'You get used to it. And I'm always in the midst of a family when I'm working. The company becomes your family. Say I'm married to the theatre.'

'I'd call that a good marriage,' she said. 'But there should be room in your life for someone else if the right person came along.'

'Maybe,' he said. 'I wouldn't know about that until I meet the right person.'

'That's true,' she said as they turned in by the playhouse and headed for the big yellow building where she was to live for the summer. He brought the car to a halt outside it.

He turned to her and said, 'Let's do this again.'

'I'd like to.'

'I want us to be good friends,' he told her, his handsome face earnest as he studied her.

'I don't know why you find me interesting,' she confessed. 'But I'm delighted that you seem to.'

'I do,' he said. 'But don't let me interfere with any fun or friendships with the others. Don't be afraid to tell me if you want to be with them instead of seeing me. That's the only basis on which we can establish a friendship.'

'I'll be frank with you,' she said. 'It will be easy. I know now I'll always prefer to see you to anyone else.'

He smiled faintly. 'I wonder.'

'I'm sure it will always be true, Tim,' she said softly. 'You don't mind my calling you Tim, do you?'

'Mind? I insist on it,' the handsome actor said as he took her in his arms for a goodnight kiss.

4

Jennifer made her way upstairs to the attic room which she shared with the other two girls in an ecstatic mood. Tim's kiss had been tender and deliciously exciting. Her head was in the clouds and she knew that no matter what she tried to tell herself she'd lost her heart to the charming leading man. As she hesitated in the dark hall before opening the door to her room she prayed that her room-mates would be asleep.

Then she cautiously opened the door and went in. Almost at once Helen stirred in her bed and reached out to turn on the small lamp on the table by her bedside. The redhead gave Jennifer a sleepy glance.

Helen said, 'We've all been in bed for ages!'

'I didn't mean to waken you,' she

apologised from the middle of the room.

Sybil was also sitting up in bed with her pretty face showing a jeering look. 'I'll bet you didn't,' she said.

Helen said, 'What do you mean, taking off with the leading man the first time you meet him?'

She laughed wryly. 'It was his idea. We went to the Colony Lounge. And I met a friend of my father's there!'

'Well! Well!' Helen mocked her. 'That old friend of your father's kept you up pretty late, didn't he?'

'I didn't realise how late it was,' she protested.

'I'll bet you didn't,' Sybil said cynically. 'Not when you were with Mr Charm himself!'

'Not only that,' Helen said, 'but you stood poor Buddy Phillips up. He saw you leave with Tim Moore and he felt so miserable he took Sybil and I to the coffee shop for an hour. So some good did come out of your bad behaviour.'

Jennifer crossed and sat on the foot

of Helen's bed. 'I'm sorry about Buddy. I didn't mean to stand him up.'

'But you did!' Sybil told her.

She glanced across the room at the brunette. 'We had only a casual arrangement. Nothing was really planned.'

Helen said, 'So you went with Tim.'

'Yes. I didn't think it was all that wrong.'

Helen shrugged. 'He's a lot older than you and he happens to be a divorced man!'

She said, 'That was ages ago! He hasn't been married for years.'

'He's still a divorced man,' Sybil said with relish. 'And, anyway, the apprentices aren't supposed to socialise with the regular company.'

'Who says so?' Jennifer wanted to know.

'It's an unwritten law,' Sybil said.

Helen looked disgusted. 'Well, if it's unwritten it doesn't count. Go out with whoever you like, Jennifer,' was the redhead's advice. 'I know Tim can be very nice.'

'He is,' she agreed. 'And he made it

perfectly clear about his divorce and being double my age. It's just that we are friends. I think he's the sort to make a wonderful friend.'

'Of course there's nothing wrong with it!' Helen agreed.

'What about Ruth Crane?' Sybil said. She was still sitting up and seemed fully awake.

'I'd forgotten about Ruth,' Helen confessed.

'Who is she?' Jennifer asked.

'She's in the professional company. In her late twenties or early thirties. She sometimes plays leads and often supporting parts.'

Sybil pointed out, 'She was in the rehearsal tonight. She has large brown eyes and streaked brownish hair.'

She at once remembered. 'Of course! She plays Tim's wife in the play.'

'That's the one,' Helen nodded.

'And she regards Tim as her particular property,' Sybil warned her. 'They say the only reason she's come back these last two years is because of him.

She has a big part in that Hollywood spy show that is so popular. They've finished taping all the television programmes for next season and that is why she's free to come here.'

'She has money, too,' Sybil pointed out. 'She has a cottage of her own down the road from here, near the golf course. She's the only one other than Roger Deering who has her own place.'

Jennifer was listening to all this with surprise. 'You say she's seriously interested in Tim?'

Helen's plain, comedienne's face was solemn as she said, 'I don't believe anyone would ever question that.'

'He can't care for her, then,' she said.

'They're friendly enough. They often play tennis together at the club.'

Jennifer protested, 'That still doesn't have to mean anything. Nor is my going out with him important. We just happen to have good chemistry for friendship.'

Helen looked wise. 'I've heard about those chemistry experiments before. Just be careful it doesn't end in a violent explosion.'

Sybil said, 'That's good advice, honey! And now, do hurry and get to bed! I'm so sleepy!' The last was a wail as the brunette lay back and covered her head with the sheets.

'I'm sorry!' Jennifer apologised, and she got up from Helen's bed quickly and went over to her own. There she hastily began to change into her night clothes.

Within a few minutes she was in bed and the room was in darkness again. She could already hear Sybil's soft snoring and Helen was silent. But she found it difficult to get to sleep. She was simply too excited. It had been a thrilling evening for her right from the rehearsal on. And she was certain that Tim Moore really had a romantic interest in her. It was a wonderful start for the summer.

After a long while she slept. It seemed almost no time until it was morning and the others were getting up. Sybil, in short shorts and a tiny pink halter, was standing by her bed regarding her with mocking derision.

'I get your type,' she said. 'Up most of the night and then never in time for breakfast in the morning!'

She sat up quickly. 'How much time have we?'

Helen called across the room, 'They stop serving breakfast in ten minutes.'

'I'll make it!' she promised, throwing aside the bedclothes and quickly swinging out to search for her slippers.

And she did! She arrived downstairs just before Mrs Thatcher shut the dining-room doors to late-comers. The big woman gave her a resigned glance and let her come into the room with its four big round tables. Most of the others had eaten and left, but Helen, Sybil and Buddy were still at the table.

As she sat down Buddy turned to her with a teasing smile. 'I didn't know if we were going to see you again. I thought you might be joining the main company at their place.'

She took this jibe with good humour.

'I'm sorry about last night,' she said. 'I didn't think we'd planned anything definite.'

'I had,' Buddy said. 'But I guess you hadn't. It's all right. Did you have a good time with old Tim?'

'I like him,' she said. 'He's very nice.'

'He's a good actor,' Buddy said, helping himself to more coffee. 'No one can deny that.'

Helen changed the subject by asking, 'What is the schedule for today?'

Buddy said, 'I'm going to be busy with Ned Chadwick, working on sets for the next play. Sybil will still be helping with the scene painting and you are to work in the box office until after lunch. The rest of the day is your own.'

'Generous!' Helen said with a grimace.

'I'm sick of those paint pots and brushes,' Sybil complained. 'I wind up with paint all over me.'

Buddy eyed her slyly. 'But that's no problem with you, honey. You usually wear so little clothing all you need to do is take a quick shower and you're fine again.'

Sybil got up from the table in disgust. 'You!'

Jennifer turned to him. 'What about me?'

'That's all planned,' he said. 'You and Two-Ton are to go out in the playhouse pick-up and deliver handbills to houses in Cape Porpoise and Biddeford Pool.'

Helen told her, 'That will keep you moving on this hot day. I'd rather be in the box office. At least there's a fan in there.'

Jennifer smiled. 'Anything to help the cause.'

'We do need to get the handbills delivered with the season starting next week,' Buddy said.

Jennifer went over to the playhouse around nine-thirty. Out back there were scenery flats stretched out on the grass, and Sybil and some other young men and women were beginning to apply paint to them under the direction of the scenic artist. Backstage Buddy and Ken

Chadwick were mapping out the set and properties for the Noel Coward play. While Helen and a young male apprentice whom Jennifer knew only as Red had installed themselves in the box office to wait for customers.

She walked along the veranda and found Randy Scott hunched behind the wheel of the pick-up truck reading a comic magazine. He hastily put it aside on seeing her and gave her one of his friendly grins.

'Ready to start out?' he asked.

'Yes,' she said. 'Do you have the handbills?'

He nodded. 'I've a whole stack of them. I'll drive and you can pass them out.'

She opened the door of the pick-up and got in on the leather seat beside him. 'It sounds to me as if you will be getting the best of the bargain.'

He started the engine. 'In a deal like this there is no best. But if we hurry we can get through in time to drive down to the wharf at Cape Porpoise and watch the boats for a while.'

'That sounds pleasantly lazy.'

'I don't intend to work every minute of the summer,' Randy said.

They drove through the village and along route number nine, where they started leaving handbills at every house. Some of the summer places were still locked up, but Jennifer slid handbills under the doors anyway. Quite a few of the regular residents whom she caught at home said they weren't interested. She accepted this as a challenge and tried to talk them into attending the first week's play. Others greeted her warmly and expressed a real enthusiasm for the theatre. She was grateful for them and usually talked with them for a little.

The stout Randy remained behind the wheel as the hot summer day advanced. The windows of the pick-up were down, but the cab was warm and he perspired a lot.

'I'll be glad when we get this all done,' he complained as he drove on to another group of houses. 'We've just got Kennebunk and the main highway left to do.'

'How long will that take?'

'Most of the rest of this week,' he grumbled. 'After that we'll be busy at the playhouse.'

She said, 'You wanted to be an actor.'

'I don't see any connection between giving out handbills and being an actor,' the fat young man said unhappily.

By the time they had finished their rounds their stock of handbills was almost exhausted. Randy then drove down to the wharf he'd mentioned which had an excellent view. There was also a large restaurant near the wharf which he claimed to be one of the best in the area. He invited her to have a sandwich with him and when she refused he went up and got one for himself. It was not hard to know why he kept so stout, she decided, he was continually eating or thinking about food.

They sat on a bench by the wharf and enjoyed the salty breeze from the ocean and the warm sunshine. Jennifer thought this was typical of the Maine climate, this mixture of the cool and warm.

As Randy finished his sandwich he turned to her and said, 'I have an idea.'

'What sort of idea?' she asked.

'You know they won't let me do any acting at the playhouse,' Randy complained.

'You can't be sure.'

'I can see how it's shaping up,' he said. 'You hear them calling me Two-Ton. They see me as a funny fat guy. The moment I step on stage people in the audience are going to laugh.'

'That will be all right,' she said, 'if they fit you in the type of part where it doesn't matter.'

'And how many parts are there like that?'

'Not many,' she admitted.

'You're right, there's not,' the stout Randy said. 'So all I do is work backstage or be a general errand boy. I'll only gain by observing.'

Jennifer looked at him earnestly. 'I guess that's about it.'

'And I want to act!'

'So?'

'That's where my idea comes in,' he said.

'Go on.'

'One of the coffee houses in the dock has a guitar player and a girl singer,' Randy explained. 'But the other one doesn't have any steady entertainment.'

'And?'

'I plan to go to them and offer to play my guitar a little and mix it with a stand-up comedy routine between tunes. I'd give a show every evening after the performance. If they want to laugh at me, let me cash in on it. I'll be a funny man.'

Jennifer laughed. 'It sounds a grand idea. And you'll be on stage every night!'

'That's the best part of it,' he agreed. 'You certainly should talk to the coffee house people,' she said.

Randy showed a smile on his round face. 'The others would make fun of me, but I knew I could tell you.'

'Of course!'

'I'm going to go talk to the manager of the coffee house tonight. If he agrees to the idea I'll plan to open the night after the playhouse opens. I'd like to invite all the cast and everyone else at the playhouse to be there.'

'I promise I'll come,' she said. 'And I'm sure Sybil and Helen will. And Buddy Phillips!'

'That would be a good start,' Randy said. And then he added, 'I think Buddy has his eye on you.'

'Oh?'

'Sure,' the fat young man said. 'I've not seen him take so much interest in a girl since we all arrived here. But the minute you turned up he was turned on.'

She laughed. 'I don't think I made that much impression.'

'You did,' Randy argued. 'Buddy can

have his pick of the girls. He's not like me. And he keeps away from most of them. But not you! I'll bet he'll be dating you before the season's over.'

'I'm here to work, not date,' she reminded him.

He grinned. 'You'll get some dating in as well unless you're a lot different from everyone else.'

After a little they got in the car and drove back to the playhouse. They had lunch and set out again. This time going to Kennebunk, where it was warmer than it had been nearer the ocean. By the time they wound up for the afternoon she was exhausted. She hoped that they would get back to the boarding house in time for her to have a short sleep before dinner. But they didn't.

As they were driving towards the playhouse a convertible with its top down came racing by them in the opposite direction. She had just time to see that Tim Moore was a passenger in the gold sports car and he was in tennis clothes. He had spotted them and waved as the vehicles passed. At the wheel of the convertible was actress Ruth Crane, also in tennis whites but with a red handkerchief tied over her brown tresses.

'Ladies and gentlemen of the ensemble,' Randy complained. 'They ride off to kill time with tennis while we drudge handing out playbills.'

She smiled. 'That's how the world is divided.'

'I don't like being in the wrong half,' was the fat man's lament.

Seeing the two together made her realise what a wide chasm there was between her world and that of the professional members of the company. And she worried about whether it would be possible for her and Tim to continue to build their friendship or whether it was merely a Quixotic dream. Only time would tell.

As the alternate to a sleep she took a brisk, cold shower which woke her up nicely for dinner. Afterwards it was back to the theatre for the seven o'clock rehearsal. In the interim she had gone over the play several times and now she felt she could be more valuable as prompter. She would be able to toss out any needed lines much faster.

Everything was a bustle backstage. She took her place and waited for the performance to begin. Tim Moore came to speak to her briefly before he went on. 'I didn't know whether you knew me when we drove by today.'

She said, 'Yes. I saw you. We were on our way back from giving out handbills.'

Tim's handsome face showed a smile. 'You make me feel guilty. Do you play tennis?'

'Not well.'

'We must try you some morning or afternoon,' he said. 'I'm not all that good myself.'

Ned Chadwick came by, crying out, 'Places, everyone!' The thin stage manager continued on and the company got ready for the rehearsal to begin.

In the beginning the run-through went well. Now that Jennifer knew who was playing Tim's wife, she took a special interest in her performance. There was no question that Ruth Crane was a crisply competent actress. She was not a great beauty, but she had a good bone structure and a lean, elegant look.

The crisis came in the second act and once again it was the guest star, Donald Winter, who brought it about. He floundered on an important line and brought a fast-moving scene to a complete halt.

From the darkened auditorium there was a howl of pain from Roger Deering. 'Not again!'

Jennifer called out the line to the upset British star, who did not seem to be hearing her but stood there with a dazed look on his thin face.

Roger Deering shouted up, 'Begin the scene again. Surely you can manage it with another try.'

Donald Winter came over to her in

the wings and asked her if he might check the prompt book. 'If I read it over maybe it will stay with me,' he said.

She gladly gave him the book while the others in that scene lounged about onstage, waiting in a bored fashion. She saw Ruth Crane and Tim Moore talking in a very earnest way and it occurred to her that they made an attractive and talented team. She did not wonder at the older actress being interested in Tim romantically.

Donald Winter finished reviewing the lines and returned onstage. The scene was rehearsed again and this time it went through without any mishap. The third act also went well and Helen and Sybil were hilariously funny in their comic roles. Even though Sybil had nothing to say, she gave the part the quality it needed in her pantomime and by her good looks. Helen had just the right comic tone for the larger role.

The rehearsal ended about ten-fifteen. Jennifer stood in the wings with her prompt book in hand and couldn't help wondering whether Tim would come to talk to her now the evening's work was at an end. She hadn't long to debate the matter as Tim suddenly came off the set with Ruth on his arm.

As they came over to her Ruth smiled at her glacially and said, 'So you're the talented young woman Tim has been raving about.'

She managed an embarrassed smile in return. 'I'm not all that talented,' she said.

'Tim seems to think so,' Ruth Crane said with a glance up at him. An intimate, amused glance.

Tim said, 'I do think Jennifer has great theatre potential.'

Ruth Crane raised an eyebrow and studied her again. 'Well, I'm sure we'll know before the season ends. I'd like to spend an hour with you now and get to know you beter, darling, but Tim and I have an invitation to a divine party at a friend's house on the beach. So I'll have to put it off until another time.' She clung to Tim's arm as she said this.

Tim gave Jennifer a troubled look and promised, 'I'll be in touch with you soon.'

'Of course,' she said in a small voice.

With that Ruth Crane offered a triumphant smile and then left, still clinging to Tim Moore's arm. It was evident she had no intention of losing the handsome leading man's company for another night.

5

'Interested in an understudy?' a voice asked in her ear.

She turned to see Buddy Phillips standing there with an amused look on his thin face. She decided to go along with the joke. 'It seems I can use one. Ruth has a firm grip on the leading man.'

'I noticed that,' Buddy said. 'You can be sure someone told her about last night.'

'You think so?'

'Sure.'

'I wouldn't consider it of that much importance,' she said.

Buddy made a face. 'You don't know the gossips we have in this company. I'm all ready to leave. I was going to suggest we go to the Forefather's Inn for a little refreshment.'

'The Forefather's Inn?' she said. 'I've

never heard of it.'

'A crowd gathers there almost every night,' Buddy said. 'It's a fun place!'

'I'd like to see it,' she said.

'Fine,' he said. 'We'll take my car. It's a couple of miles back of here on the road that joins on to the main road.'

'Sounds suitably isolated,' she laughed.

'It is. But there's plenty of action when you get there!'

He proved right. The Forefather's Inn was an ancient, rambling post house whose rooms had been converted into a large bar and restaurant. In the main big room a rock band blared forth their loud brand of entertainment and a host of mini-skirted and sport-shirted youngsters jumped and pranced to the strong beat. They chose one of the smaller, dimly lighted quiet rooms where they could relax and talk at their table.

After they were served he stared across the table and said, 'You looked lost when Ruth dragged Tim off tonight.'

'Did I?'

'Yes. I felt sorry for you. I was also a little surprised. You have only known him a couple of days. You can't have fallen in love with him in so short a time.'

She smiled. 'Are you determined to psychoanalyse me?'

'Say, I'm concerned about you.'

'Thanks.'

'I mean it.'

'I'm sure you do,' she said. She gave him a thoughtful look. 'You want me to tell you about Tim and how I feel about him? That isn't going to be easy.'

Buddy Phillips smiled. 'We have all the rest of the night.'

'In that case I suppose I'd better try,' she said. 'I'd rather talk about you, though.'

'I can wait,' the young man said.

'All right. What do I feel about Tim Moore? I think he is someone very special. I look up to him as a Broadway player. And because he's older he's sort of a father figure as well as a male who interests me romantically. That's a fatal combination where a female is concerned.'

'It sounds it.'

'I think I need someone like him at this time of my life,' she went on seriously. 'I don't mean we have to have a wonderful love affair or get married or anything like that. I just need his influence, his advice and his kindness. I haven't received too much of it from my own father.'

'Ah!' Buddy said. 'That does make you vulnerable.'

She glanced down and toyed with the handle of her cup. 'I suppose so.'

'I'd be afraid it might turn out to be a dangerous game for you,' the young man warned her.

'Why?'

'I think your feelings are deeper than you guess,' he told her. 'I'd say you could wind up falling deeply in love with Tim and he with you. He's at an age and time in his career when he may need someone like you just as much as you think you need him. You might both wind up mistakenly believing a marriage between you would solve all your problems.'

She gave him a challenging glance. 'And why not?'

He shook his head. 'You're already on your way to trouble.'

'Not necessarily,' she said. 'But tell me why, if Tim and I decided to marry, it would be a mistake.'

Buddy took a deep breath and sat back. 'All right,' he said. 'For starters Tim Moore has to be forty-five if he's a day!'

'He's the Cary Grant type,' she said. 'He's probably more charming now than he was at twenty.'

'He is also a quarter-century older, and if that sounds bad, it is,' Buddy warned her. 'Maybe you need a husband a little older than yourself, but that's a lot of difference.'

'I call it a weak reason for protesting such a marriage,' she said. 'What are the others?'

'Tim Moore isn't all that successful. Sure, he's been in some Broadway shows and he's played here a long while. But he hasn't really made it and now the tide could turn against him. He is apt to wind up having a hard time making a living in show business.'

This came as a surprise to her. She had only thought of Tim as a very successful actor. His experience had awed her and his having been on Broadway. She said, 'Why should he have career trouble now?'

'To be blunt, he's an over-the-hill leading man,' Buddy said seriously. 'And there are more of them around than you think. My father employs a lot of them in his dinner-theatre operations because they are minor names and he can get them cheap.'

'I'm sure Tim will always find work,' she insisted.

'I've heard stories about his being out of work for long periods before this,' the young man warned her. 'It is bound to happen again, and as he get's older it is sure to be worse. Unless you have money or really make it, acting can be a cruel business as you get old.'

'Tim Moore isn't old!'

'Ageing,' Buddy said firmly.

She smiled wanly. 'All right, ageing.'

'We have examples of old actors in trouble here in this company,' he said. 'You saw R. Dudley Moffet play that funny bank examiner part.'

'Yes. He's very good.'

'And he's losing his eyesight,' Buddy said. 'He can just see enough light and shadow to find his way around the stage. He pretends to be a lot better than he is so people won't notice. This job is terribly important to him. He has one of the other actors read his lines to him and cue him and Ned Chadwick had me go all over the stage with him as he worked out the various exits and furniture from memory. Otherwise he'd be apt to stumble and fall.'

She was amazed. 'I had no idea!'

'He's a game old fellow,' Buddy said. 'But he's a victim of this business. How much longer can he hope to work?'

'You're trying to depress me,' she told him.

'I want you to see that the theatre is not all glamour, little dramatic school graduate.'

'That's mean!' she protested.

'Sorry,' he said. 'I imagine no matter what I say or how much I warn you it will make no difference. You'll go on building a friendship with Tim.'

'I think so,' she said frankly. 'He's offered to help me with a part in a play that is coming up.'

'There is nothing wrong with that. He has the ability to help you.'

She smiled. 'And I enjoy his company.'

Buddy leaned forward on the table. 'You'll get some problems from Ruth Crane if you see much of him. She considers him her special property.'

'And I understand she is very successful.'

'She has been. She's no star, but she's in demand. If she married Tim she might be able to help him. At least she'd be working at a good salary if he happened to be idle.'

'I can't see Tim wanting that.'

'He doesn't,' Buddy agreed. 'I'm sure of it. But that doesn't mean he knows what's good for him.'

She lifted her eyebrows. 'And you think you do?'

'At least I can be objective. That's something.'

She said accusingly, 'And as the son of a wealthy man in show business you don't have to worry about your future.'

'Ah!' he said with a mocking smile. 'I'm glad you brought that up.'

'Are you?'

'You'd be surprised if you knew how many people cater to me because they think I'm in a position to help them with jobs,' he said.

'You mean they are that obvious?'

'They are,' he said with disgust. 'It's the one thing that has bothered me. I wish the members of the playhouse company didn't know who I am. But it's too late to hide it now. They have me tagged.'

'You still are lucky. Your father has an important job for you when you finish here.'

He looked at her very directly. 'Want to know something?'

'What?'

'I'm not going to take his job,' Buddy Phillips said. 'He's in for a surprise. I've been coming to this decision for a long time. Whatever I do I intend to make it on my own.'

She gasped. 'But the whole point of your being here is to learn more about stage producing so you can head up your father's dinner-theatre chain.'

'That's his plan. He's been making plans for me all my life,' Buddy said. 'When I leave here I'm going to New York to pound the streets for the best stage manager job I can find. And I'll find it on my own.'

Jennifer stared at him. Then she laughed. 'So all the people who are toadying up to you are wasting their time.'

'Every minute of it,' he said happily. 'Isn't that great? My father won't even be speaking to me after he hears what I'm planning to do.'

'I guess they deserve it,' she decided. 'But I don't feel that you do. Why make things hard for yourself?'

'A matter of pride,' he said. 'If and when I go back to my father for work, I want to have a lot more experience to offer than I have now.'

'I think I understand,' she said.

Before they could continue their conversation the British star, Donald Winter, appeared in the room where they were seated. He recognised them at once and came over to their table.

'Buddy,' he said, and then smiled at her, 'and my prompt lady.'

'Won't you sit down?' Buddy invited the older man as he stood to greet him.

'For a moment,' the star said, sinking into an empty chair. 'I have just come from a party attended by most of the cast. Given by a stout lady with a large home. I found the company boring and I tired of the drinks so I left.'

She asked, 'Were Tim Moore and Ruth Crane there?'

'Very much so,' he said. 'I believe they were still there when I left, but I couldn't be sure. Roger had to attend because the old lady is one of the theatre's chief backers and he daren't offend her.'

Buddy smiled. 'It's a very complicated business.'

'Yes,' Donald Winter said bleakly. 'I shall be glad when the week's run is ended and I can return to my television chores.'

'I've always enjoyed you on television,' Jennifer said.

He eyed her with interest. 'It is my chief medium.' Then he glanced out the doorway to the room where the orchestra was playing. 'That is an extraordinarily loud band,' he declared.

'I know,' she agreed. 'We were just saying that.'

The droll face of the British star showed interest. 'But the beat is solid! Would you care to dance with me, prompt lady?' He was already on his feet with his hand out for her to rise.

She could not refuse him. 'Very well,' she said, rising. 'Excuse us, Buddy.'

Buddy was laughing. 'Have fun and don't come back deaf!'

Donald Winter proudly marched her out to the raised dance platform. A few of the young people there recognised him and she could feel the interest in the room. They took their places on the crowded dance floor and solemnly went through the ritual of jogging up and down a foot from each other, which seemed to be the mode of dancing indulged in by the crowds attending.

They kept at it until the music ended and then left the platform breathless. The British Donald Winter said, 'A most unusual experience. I must remember it.'

He took her back to their table and said goodnight and then left the busy inn. She found herself sitting with a thoroughly amused Buddy.

Buddy said, 'I'm surprised that he made it through the dance. You tired him out!'

'It was his idea,' she reminded him.

'So it was,' the young man said. 'Had enough excitement for the night?'

'I've had fun!'

'We'll do it again,' Buddy promised. 'And there are some other interesting places.'

'I'm sure there are,' she said.

They drove back to the boarding house and he parked his car. It was a pleasant, warm night and they strolled across the theatre parking lot to the big yellow house.

She said, 'I don't see any lights in the windows.'

'We're the last ones in,' he guessed. 'Most of them sleep well here. They like to go to bed early.'

'It's the air and the hard work,' she agreed. 'I feel really sleepy now.'

They paused on the doorstep for a

last glance at the stars. Buddy said, 'Thanks for a fun evening.'

She turned to him with a smile. 'And thank you for all the lectures and revelations.'

'You'll have forgotten them by the morning,' he predicted.

'I hope so,' she said.

'You look very young and lovely,' he said with an unexpected warmth in his voice. 'Goodnight, Jennifer.' He took her in his arms for a goodnight kiss. It did not thrill her as Tim Moore's kiss had, but it was a pleasant enough experience.

As they parted, she said softly, 'Goodnight, Buddy.'

Then they went inside together and with youthful high spirits struggled with repressed laughter as they stumbled up the dark stairs and made their way groping along the corridors to their respective rooms.

When she reached the room she shared with Helen and Sybil it was in darkness again. But this time neither of the girls woke up when she entered. So she prepared for bed very quietly and was able to get between the sheets without being exposed to a third degree. A few minutes later she, also, was asleep.

In the morning both girls were full of questions about where she'd gone and what had happened. When she told them about her dance with star Donald Winter they were astonished.

'Imagine him going to a place like the Forefather's Inn!' Helen exclaimed as they all dressed for breakfast. 'He's such a quiet little man!'

Sybil was in front of the mirror doing some last-minute arranging of her long, dark hair. 'I guess Jennifer cured his quietness,' she said.

'It was he who wanted to dance,' Jennifer told them. 'And then it went on so long he was completely tired out. He left afterwards.'

Sybil finished with her hair and came over to her to ask, 'Well, who is your favourite date, Buddy or Tim?'

'That's an unfair question,' she protested. 'I happen to like them both in different ways!'

Helen caught her friend by the arm and said, 'Don't waste time asking silly questions or we'll be locked out of the breakfast-room. Of course she likes Tim the best! Why bother asking her!'

Jennifer gave them no satisfaction on that point but followed them down to breakfast. As a matter of fact she wasn't sure just how she felt herself. Tim Moore had truly swept her off her feet with his charm that first night they met, but now, after some sober consideration of the things Buddy had said, she wasn't nearly so sure about him.

After breakfast they were given their assignments for the day and she was posted to the ticket office, while Helen was sent out in the pick-up with Randy Scott to continue distributing the handbills. Helen groaned at this, but Jennifer was pleased to be put in the box office.

Sybil shared the job of selling tickets with her and since they were now getting near the opening night, there was an almost steady stream of cars drawing up with people wanting to buy tickets. Some of them bought season's tickets, which gave them a slight discount.

Mid-way in the morning producer Roger Deering came to join them in the box office. He was casually dressed in slacks and white shirt open at the neck. He still had a very theatrical air about him, although he had not appeared on the stage himself for a number of years.

He checked the number of tickets left for the opening show and registered satisfaction. 'Almost a sell-out, girls,' he commented.

Jennifer smiled at him between customers and said, 'We've had a big run this morning. Just some scattered seats in the front section left and a few at the back.'

'So I see,' Roger Deering said with a

bright expression illuminating his actor-ish face. 'And let me tell you here is where it is all decided as well as on the stage. If we don't do well here it makes no difference what the performance is like.'

Sybil said, 'A lot of the people here this morning spoke about the Ogunquit show. Shirley Booth is playing there next week.'

Roger Deering frowned. 'Stiff opposition! And I've paid a good penny for Donald Winter. That's where Ogunquit is pounding us. It's because of the packages. They get a new, big star every week and we can't afford that.'

The conversation was ended when more customers arrived, but Jennifer remembered what he said. It was in line with what Tim Moore had told her earlier. The package productions were taking over most of the summer playhouses.

She and Sybil remained in the box office until after lunch. They were then entitled to the rest of the day off. Sybil already had a date to go to the private beach club at Kennebunk with a young local man. Jennifer was undecided what she would do. She considered washing her hair and gave that idea up. She was about to go out and sunbathe when Mrs Thatcher called upstairs to tell her she was wanted on the phone.

The phone was in the lower hallway of the boarding house and she ran all the way down. She was breathless when she got there. Picking up the phone, she gasped, 'Yes?'

'Did you run all the way?' an amused voice asked.

'As a matter of fact I did,' she said, recognising the pleasant voice of leading man Tim Moore.

'Sorry,' he said.

'It's all right.'

'I've found a script of 'Come Back Tomorrow' among my things,' he said. 'I'd like to give it to you. I want you to read it early and be very familiar with it.'

She was at once excited. 'That is kind of you!'

'Not at all,' he said. 'I'm going to the Colony pool for a swim. Would you care to join me? I can give you the script then.'

'I'd love it,' she said. 'I have the afternoon off.'

'Fine,' Tim said. 'I'll be over to pick you up in about ten minutes.'

'I'll be waiting for you downstairs.' she said.

She quickly put the phone back down and ran upstairs to her room again. From then on it was a rush to find the bathing suit she thought would best do for the occasion, then a bathing cap which had mysteriously vanished to be found under some other things, and a suitable beach dress to wear over everything. She had no idea how they approached the Colony pool, but she knew she'd need something for walking in and out of the lobby is they had to use that way.

At last she was ready. She surveyed

herself in the yellow and black floral beach dress in the long mirror and decided she looked all right. And she smiled at her reflection, thinking how very excited she was at the prospect of being with Tim again.

6

Tim did not keep her waiting. He drove up in his sporty black foreign car exactly on time. When she got in beside him she saw he was wearing plaid slacks and a knitted white shirt open at the neck. She thought he looked younger and more handsome than she'd ever seen him before. His dark complexion and tanned skin stood out against the white of his shirt.

'I'm glad you were able to join me,' he said, swinging the car around and heading in the direction of the village again.

She smiled. 'You hit me on a lucky day. I worked in the box office this morning and so I have the afternoon off.'

'Great!' he said. 'We can stop by the Colony pool for a while and then drive on somewhere quieter if we like. I am able to enjoy privileges at the pool because I have friends staying there. They can invite guests.'

'That is convenient.'

'I take advantage of it whenever I can,' he told her as they drove along a quiet back street which would eventually enable them to reach the hotel. The street was lined with stately old elms and Victorian-looking large houses, some of which had been turned into tourist homes.

They took a narrow road and turned to the right and arrived at the big white hotel by a different route. This time they had to park in a big lot across the street from the main building. They walked over to the cool, shadowed lobby and registered at the desk for pool privileges. Tim Moore gave the name of his friends and paid the required fee. Then he and Jennifer went down to the dressing-rooms to change into their bathing suits and go out to the pool which was set high on a rock foundation overlooking the ocean.

'What a marvellous view!' she exclaimed. 'I didn't fully appreciate it the other night when we were here.'

'You can see a long way out across the ocean and all of the Kennebunk beach area,' the handsome leading man said as they stood with their beach bags in hand.

She eyed the many deck chairs around the sparkling, mammoth pool and asked him, 'Where do you want to locate?'

He was wearing dark glasses and now he strained to see in the bright glare of the sun. 'My friends said they'd save chairs for us. They generally sit down on the left.' He stared in that direction and then added with satisfaction, 'I see them now!'

They walked down the concrete patio which surrounded the pool on all sides. Hotel guests were stretched out sunning themselves in bathing suits; some sat on the chairs in conversation, a few were splashing about in the pool and some youngsters were using the diving board and shrilly screaming as they dived down into the water.

Tim's friends proved to be an elderly couple, James and Ellen Hanley of Philadelphia. They were people of small stature but had the distinctive look of the cultured wealthy. They proved young in manner and although not dressed for bathing, were quite at home sunning themselves by the pool in smart summer sports outfits.

Ellen Hanley wore a big aqua straw hat with a wide brim to protect her pleasant if somewhat wrinkled face from the sun. She insisted that Jennifer sit beside her and at once began asking her about her theatre experience. At the same time James Hanley talked with Tim. It seemed he had once been a contractor and Tim's father had been the architect for many of his buildings.

Ellen Hanley told Jennifer, 'Tim's father was very disappointed when he went into the theatre. He wanted him to join him in the family business. But I guess it has worked out all right. Tim seems to be happy in his profession.'

'I'm sure of that,' she said.

The old woman lowered her voice so they would not be easily overheard by her husband and Tim on the bench in front of them. 'I do think that Tim made a great financial sacrifice in his choice,' she said. 'His younger brother received most of his father's money. Both parents have been dead quite a little while and I would suspect that Tim has gone through whatever was left him.'

'I don't think he places that much value on money,' she said.

Ellen Hanley nodded. 'He's probably wise in that. Though it can be important as one gets older.'

Tim came to interrupt the conversation by smiling and asking, 'Want to try the water?'

'Why not?' she said. She put on her bathing cap and they went to the shallow end of the pool and stepped down in. The water was heated to a comfortable temperature and within a few minutes they were swimming its length and thoroughly enjoying it. They both were reasonably good swimmers and so they stayed in the water for nearly twenty minutes.

When they returned to the deck chairs the Hanleys were on the point of leaving. They shook hands with her and expressed a wish to see her again. When they returned to the hotel she and Tim were left alone by the pool. The children who'd been diving had also vanished somewhere and so it was quiet out there.

They stretched out on the deck chairs side by side to enjoy the sun. Tim said sleepily, 'This is the life! It's the main reason I enjoy summer theatre.'

'I can see its benefits,' she agreed.

'The Hanleys were friends of my parents,' he said.

'They are nice people. And attractive for their age,' she said.

'Exceptionally so,' he agreed. He sat up on an elbow and smiled across at her. 'I have a sneaking idea they think I ruined my life by being an actor. They're very conservative.'

She returned his smile. 'Don't you enjoy having people concerned about your welfare?'

'No,' he said. 'But I do think they are good friends.'

They relaxed for perhaps another twenty minutes and then he rummaged in his beach bag and brought out the script. 'I want you to take this home with you. Be sure to study it. When you've read it thoroughly I'm going to give you some special coaching in the part of Ann.'

'Thank you,' she said gratefully as she took the blue-bound script. 'When is this play scheduled to be done?'

'It will be the third production,' he said. 'So you haven't all that much time to spare.'

'I'll get right at it,' she promised, flipping the pages of the bulky script.

'The part is small but an excellent one,' he assured her. 'And if I have anything to say about it you'll be playing it.'

She gave him an embarrassed smile. 'I don't want you to try and push me. Let me see if I can get it on my own.'

'I'll do that,' he promised. 'But I do want to coach you. Then we'll see what Roger Deering thinks about you.'

She asked, 'Will you be playing the lead?'

'I will be in this production,' he said. 'But I didn't on Broadway. I then played the part of the reporter. It's sort of a cameo, but it's a part that every director casts carefully.'

The afternoon wore on. They went in the pool once again and returned to sunbathe. Many of the deck chairs were now deserted and they had the pool almost to themselves. They got up from their chairs and went to the iron railing overlooking the road below and the ocean and beach beyond. Tim made a heroic figure standing there with his hair rustling in the breeze.

There was an air of thoughtfulness about him as he turned to her and said, 'I can't tell you why. But when I'm with you I feel at perfect peace with myself.'

'I'm glad,' she said. 'I'm always happy when I'm with you.'

'I don't understand it,' he said, baffled. 'We've only known each other such a short time and yet it seems that we've always been friends.'

She nodded. 'I know.'

'I've been getting along very well on my own,' Tim told her. 'Now suddenly I feel the need of someone. I'm only truly contented when I'm with you.'

Her eyes sparkled with joy. 'I'm glad you've said that,' she told him. 'I have exactly the same feelings about you.'

His bronzed hand reached out to cover her hand on the railing. His eyes met hers earnestly. 'But this is crazy!' he protested. 'We have no reason and surely no right to fall in love!'

'Can we chart such things?' she wanted to know.

'I suppose not,' he admitted. 'But I'm old enough to be your father.'

'But you're not my father,' she said quietly. 'And I don't feel at all like your daughter. I see you as a terribly interesting man.'

'And you're the most attractive girl I've ever known,' he said earnestly. 'And I think you have a genuine potential in the theatre.'

'So what is wrong with us falling in love?'

He sighed. 'I may as well tell you, since you'll hear anyway. A theatrical company is like a family, gossip about its members is always being passed around. I've been dating Ruth Crane quite a lot. It goes back a few years.'

'I know. She's a fine actress.'

'Very good,' he agreed. 'Today I broke an engagement with her to be with you. I think she knows why I broke it, too. And I'm sure she can't understand my acting this way. How can she, when I don't know why myself?'

Jennifer smiled wistfully. 'If what we have is so good, why question it?'

'I like that philosophy,' he said. 'But I know we're going to have some

119

opposition. Roger Deering especially frowns on any close friendships between the apprentices and the regular company. He'll have something to say.'

'I don't mind,' she said. 'Do you?'

He gave a small, bitter laugh. 'No. The truth is I'll enjoy flaunting our friendship in front of him. It's crazy, but that's the way I feel.' His hand pressed hard on hers.

'I've tried to deny that I care for you so much,' she said. 'But it hasn't worked. So why not admit it and enjoy it?'

The handsome Tim studied her tenderly. 'I hope it will be a wonderful summer for us.'

'How can it help not be?' she asked. 'It's already started that way!'

When he drove her back to the boarding house he leaned over and kissed her a tender parting kiss before she left the car. She stood and waved after the sports car as it headed back towards the 'Homestead' where the regular company lived. She then turned to enter the screen door when Randy Scott suddenly came out. The stout youth showed a broad smile as he saw her.

'I've been looking for you,' he said.

'Have you?' she smiled. 'I've been away having a swim.'

He noted her beach dress. 'So I see. I wanted to tell you about my seeing the coffee house about doing a comedy and music act for them.'

'Oh, yes!' she said, at once interested. 'How did you make out?'

'They want me,' he said happily. 'I gave them an idea of the act and strummed my guitar for them and I'm in!'

'I'm so pleased for you!' Jennifer said sincerely.

'I knew you'd be,' he agreed. 'The money isn't all that big, but I'll be working every night. And there's one more important thing. They want me to work a girl into the act.'

'Oh?'

The fat young man said, 'Yes. Sort of

a comedy foil for me. I sing to her and she pays no attention. Then I go into my comedy routine and she keeps looking disgusted. After that I break into a catchy love song and she surprises everyone by joining in singing with me. And that's the end of the act.'

She said, 'It sounds all right.'

He hesitated awkwardly. 'What I wanted to ask you is will you be the girl?'

Jennifer was surprised. 'I don't know,' she said. 'I'm not the type. You want somebody who is a comedienne. Why not Helen?'

Randy suddenly looked forlorn. 'She'd never do it! She just sees me as Two-Ton the oaf!'

'I don't think that's entirely true.'

'Sure it is. You're the only one who believes in me.'

She said, 'Why don't you let me talk to Helen about it? And then if she shows any interest you and she can discuss it.'

The stout youth brightened. 'Would

you speak to her?'

'I'll be glad to,' she said.

He looked glum again. 'I don't think she'll want to go into any act with me.'

'Don't be too sure,' Jennifer said. 'And if you could get her to join you she'd be great. I'm sure she'd help put you and the act over.'

Randy said, 'You won't consider it?'

'Not unless Helen refuses,' she said. 'I'll talk to her about it as soon as I see her.'

She hurried upstairs and found her two roommates had got back ahead of her. Helen was stretched out on her bed complaining about the exertions of passing out handbills all afternoon. Sybil had just finished showering after a session of scene painting and she was now sitting on her bed in a short dressing robe, doing her nails.

Helen sat up lazily and asked Jennifer, 'Where have you been?'

She smiled. 'At the Colony pool.'

'Listen to her!' Helen grumbled. 'She plays while we work!'

'Who took you to the pool?' Sybil wanted to know.

'Tim. He has friends staying there. We had a great afternoon,' she said.

'I'll bet!' Helen said. 'And I spent the afternoon in the pick-up with Two-Ton spreading out those handbills. To make it worse he was in one of his silent, stupid moods. He hardly heard anything I said to him.'

Jennifer sat on her bed. 'I can tell you why. He was worried.'

'Two-Ton worried? What about?' Helen wanted to know.

She said, 'You don't appreciate him. He's really a very nice, sensitive person. He's just been hired to do a nightly act at one of the coffee houses. They apparently recognised his talents. And what is worrying him is where to find a girl partner for the act.'

'I don't believe it!' Helen said.

'It's so,' she went on. 'I think it could be a great chance for someone with a sense of comedy and I suggested you!'

'Me!' Helen exclaimed. 'Play in an

act with Two-Ton?'

'Why not? It would be great experience, and I think he has a lot of promise,' Jennifer said.

'You do it!' Helen told her.

'I'm not that good at comedy,' she said.

'Then let him try Sybil,' Helen said. 'With her figure the audience won't care whether she can act or not.'

Sybil looked up from doing her nails. 'I wouldn't think of taking a job that would keep me working every night after the performance here. I've a boyfriend in Kennebunk and he expects me to give him some time.'

Helen rolled her eyes. 'Romance is raising its ugly head and skipping me as usual!'

'So make up for it by going into Randy's act,' Jennifer urged her. 'He wants you but he's too shy to ask you himself. He wanted me to broach it to you first.'

They talked about it some more and it ended with Helen grudgingly agreeing to discuss it with Randy. Jennifer felt this was a victory. She was sure if the two got together planning the act the redheaded comedienne would go through with it.

For her own part she was walking on air following her afternoon at the pool with Tim. He had finally come out with what amounted to a declaration of love for her and she had been equally frank with him. The fact that they had come to care for each other was now in the open between them. At least this was something she felt they could build on.

She briefly looked over the script of 'Come Back Tomorrow' and saw that Ann was indeed an excellent role if a short one. And she determined carefully to read and study the play as Tim had advised her.

That night the rehearsal went very smoothly. After it was over Tim came to her and, smiling down at her, said, 'My favourite prompt girl hadn't much to do tonight.'

'No. The show went very well,' she said.

He hesitated. 'Roger Deering is having a little party for Donald Winter at the Shawmut Hotel. I wondered if you'd like to come.'

'Is it for all the company?' she asked.

'For all the company,' he said carefully.

She caught something in his tone and said, 'But I'd be the only one from the apprentice group?'

The handsome leading man nodded. 'That's right. Roger hasn't invited the apprentices to this. But you'd be coming as my personal guest. I'd like to have you there.'

'I don't know,' she worried.

'You needn't worry about the others being upset since they'll know you're attending as my guest.'

She gave him a questioning look. 'What will Roger Deering have to say?'

'Nothing. Why should he?'

'You told me how he feels about apprentices and members of the company mingling.'

Tim smiled. 'Let us be the exception?

How long will it take you to slip on a party dress?'

'Fifteen minutes,' she said.

'That's good,' the leading man told her. 'I'll come by for you.'

She hurried back to the boarding house and changed quickly. Both Helen and Sybil were out somewhere. She'd seen Helen and Randy talking earlier in the evening and she hoped they might be seeing each other and settling plans for the coffee house act. After she'd selected the white halter-neck dress which seemed the best bet for the party, she quickly made up.

When she reached the doorstep of the boarding house there was still no sign of Tim's car. A figure loomed out of the shadows and it proved to be Buddy Phillips on his way back from the playhouse. Still in his backstage work clothes, he halted by her.

'Going to the party at the Shawmut?' he asked.

'Yes.'

He said, 'I didn't know any of the

apprentice company were invited.'

'Tim is taking me.'

'I see!' he exclaimed. 'Special guest! Good luck to you! I think it will be a good party.'

His good nature about it all somehow made her ashamed. She said, 'I wish everyone were coming. It makes me feel awkward being the only one.'

'You're older than a lot of the apprentice group,' Buddy said. 'You'll fit in over there where some of the kids wouldn't. They'd only be bored.'

'I suppose that's true,' she said with a sigh.

Just then Tim drove up and she left the young backstage worker to get into the sports car. When she entered the car she discovered the character man, R. Dudley Moffet, was seated in the front seat beside the leading man.

Tim said, 'Dudley had no way of getting to the party, so I offered him a lift. We can make room for three here, can't we?'

'Of course,' she said, closing the

door. 'Good evening, Mr Moffet.'

'Good evening, my dear,' the old character actor said in his courtly way. He was a big man with a mass of white hair framing a distinguished face. Offstage he always wore thick, horn-rimmed glasses, and even these were not much help to him. 'I'm sorry to force my company on you two.'

'Not at all,' Tim said cheerily. 'We're all going to the same party, why shouldn't we travel together?'

During the short drive along the dark roads they managed some sort of conversation. At last they reached the Shawmut Inn parking lot and left the car to stroll across to the rambling modern hotel. Lights were blazing in every one of the large public rooms and sounds of music and merriment were already coming from its windows.

They entered the glass-walled vestibule and mounted the red carpeted stairs to the lobby. At R. Dudley Moffet's request she took his arm and guided the near-blind man safely up the steps and inside. They crossed the lobby to the lounge and she saw that it and the adjoining room were filled with people. Roger Deering had undoubtedly invited many of the influential town people as guests.

She and Tim and the old character actor strolled into the room where Roger Deering and the board members were greeting guests along with Donald Winter. Standing in the line of board members was the Shawmut Hotel owner and her father's friend, Fred Short. At the sight of her there with Tim Moore a shadow of a frown crossed his face.

7

The orchestra was a three-man group which Fred Short regularly brought in from Sanford for weekends and special events. They played well for the party, and after Jennifer had danced with Tim Moore several times she went out on the veranda facing the ocean with the handsome leading man at her side.

She stood there in the semi-darkness with him, the sound of music and conversation coming clearly from inside. Looking up at him, she said, 'Thanks for inviting me to a marvellous party!'

He nodded. 'It has been fun so far. But mostly because you're here.'

'I hope no one complains about it,' she said, a trifle worried.

'Don't give it a thought.' Tim said, brushing the idea away.

They talked for a while, mostly about the play which she'd just read, and then returned to the dancing. There was a light buffet afterwards and it was almost one-thirty when Tim drove her back to the boarding house. This time they were riding alone as R. Dudley Moffet had left earlier with someone else.

Tim kissed her goodnight tenderly. 'A night I won't soon forget,' he said.

'Nor will I,' she agreed.

She hurried upstairs and managed to get to bed without waking the others. Both Helen and Sybil were discreet in the morning and did not ask her any questions about the party. Neither did Buddy Phillips, though he enlisted her to help him line up props for the play. They used another of the theatre's pick-up trucks and went from store to store getting items of furniture, paintings and other bric-à-brac to decorate the setting.

As they drove along between stops he talked to her in a general way. 'How do you feel about the playhouse now?' he asked her.

'I've never had such a wonderful time!' she said.

He gave her a brief side-glance as they drove along the main street. 'Is that because of the playhouse or because of Tim Moore?'

Jennifer's cheeks flamed. 'That isn't a nice thing to say!'

'I'm being honest.'

'I'm enjoying everything here,' she protested. 'Tim Moore just happens to be part of it.'

Buddy's eyes were on the traffic policeman who had stopped them to allow a crowd of tourists to meander across the street. He said, 'I think you should be careful not to lose sight of why you came here. What you do at the playhouse should be most important to you. Not what you do socially.'

'I am here to work seriously,' she said, a little angry.

'I'm glad,' the young man said as the policeman gave them a signal to proceed, and he drove the car on across the bridge in the general direction of Kennebunk.

They stopped by the Narragansett Hotel to get a special large plant in a brass stand which the stage manager had picked out as a necessary part of the set decoration. Since it was a warm, sunny day, Buddy suggested they park the pick-up by the beach and take a half-hour to themselves. It sounded like a good idea to Jennifer and they left the pick-up and went down on the beach. They were fortunate enough to find a fairly isolated area, and Buddy took off his shirt and sat with the upper half of his tanned body fully exposed to the warm rays of the sun. She stretched out on the sand beside him.

He said, 'Maybe I'll have a chance to visit you in Boston or where you are teaching. I'll be in New England and in New York in the autumn.'

She let some loose sand dribble through her fingers. 'I may not teach after all.'

'Why not?'

She shrugged. 'I could change my plans. You're going to change yours, you said.'

Buddy smiled. 'I'm going to skip Dad's plans to work me into his organisation until I feel ready for it. But you have no problems like that.'

'I have my own problems,' she replied. 'I'm not all that fond of teaching. Maybe I can get a Broadway part.'

He eyed her shrewdly. 'Is Tim Moore giving you those ideas?'

'No. They're my own.'

'I hope so.'

'They are!'

Buddy glanced out at the ocean. 'It's easy to get carried away by romantic notions in a place like this. But you might find it different when you moved to a place like New York and started trying to find parts.'

She sat up and gave him a pleading look. 'Buddy, why must you preach to me? Can't we be friends without that?'

'Sure,' he said. 'And I don't mean to

preach. It's just that I think you're a great girl and I'm afraid Tim is using his position in the company to sweep you off your feet.'

'I'm having fun with him,' she said. 'Is it wrong for us to enjoy ourselves?'

Buddy shook his head. 'Not at all. Just so long as you don't create a make-believe romance which neither of you can live up to in the end. Tim is an ageing actor and you're just a youngster starting out in the theatre life. You have to watch out being tricked by false glamour.'

She gave him a bitter smile. 'And why are you so worried about me?'

Buddy's eyes met hers earnestly. 'I think because I'm fond of you,' he said. 'It could be that I've fallen in love with you.'

Jennifer was thoroughly startled by this unexpected declaration. She gasped! 'Now who is being carried away by romantic surroundings?' she demanded.

Buddy shrugged. 'I'm telling you how I feel. I can't argue about why I feel as I do.'

'Then you're jealous of Tim and I?'

'Probably,' the sandy-haired young man said. 'I think he is being selfish in leading you on as he is.'

'I'm the one who's pursuing him,' she protested.

'In that case he should discourage it,' Buddy said. 'I think it's great for you to be friends. But seriously to fall in love would be a disaster.'

Her expression was pert, 'You have it all figured out.'

'More or less. Don't be angry with me.'

She said, 'You're making it hard for me not to be.'

'I won't mention it again,' he promised.

'I'd appreciate that,' she said.

The young man smiled at her. 'On one condition.'

'What is the condition?' she asked.

'That you see me socially once in a while. Just to keep a healthy balance.'

Jennifer smiled at him incredulously. 'That's quite a lot you are asking.'

'Is my company so unpleasant?'

'No.'

'Well then?'

She hesitated, then she rubbed her hand in the loose sand as she speculated, 'I would be afraid of hurting Tim. Of making him feel ridiculous. I mean, how would he feel? I'd be dating him part of the time and then dating a younger man. It would seem that I was deliberately playing you against each other.'

'I doubt that.'

'It's a possibility.'

'Only if you and he are both serious, and I can't think that you would want to be,' Buddy argued. 'The best way to stop gossip getting started in the company is to date someone else occasionally. And it might as well be me. We have a long season ahead. You'd be protecting both yourself and Tim.'

She smiled wanly. 'You argue well.'

'I'm offering you the facts.'

'I'd enjoy dating you occasionally,' she said. 'It happens that I do like you.'

Buddy said, 'Then there's no problem.'

'Not unless you make one.'

'We're having tonight off before dress rehearsal tomorrow night,' he said. 'I'd like to take you over to a place at Perkins' Cove. What about it?'

Again she hesitated. 'I haven't heard from Tim yet. I don't know what he plans to do tonight.'

'It shouldn't matter,' Buddy said stubbornly. 'You've been with him several nights. Time to play it cool.'

She listened to the young man's arguments and knew there were sound ideas in them. Finally, she said, 'All right. Just to prove you're wrong about Tim and me, I'll go out with you tonight.'

She said this, half-hoping he wouldn't hold her to it, but she had an idea that he might. They left the beach and went back to collecting the props for the play. It was lunch time before she reached the boarding house. A number of the apprentices were stretched out on the green lawn in front of the yellow house enjoying the sun. Sybil, in one of her abbreviated bikinis, was one of them.

Sybil hailed Jennifer and said, 'You've certainly started something.'

'What?' she asked, innocently.

The dark girl smiled. 'Two-Ton and Helen have been rehearsing material for their night club act. They were over in the playhouse most of the morning.'

'I'm glad,' she said. 'It could be an important break for them.'

Sybil's pretty face showed a baffled expression. 'I never expected Helen to take Two-Ton seriously. But she is.'

'And she should. I think he's a talent.'

'I guess maybe we didn't pay enough attention to him,' the shapely brunette in the bikini commented.

'I'm sure of that,' Jennifer said.

She went upstairs and showered before lunch. Then she spent the afternoon resting and studying the script of 'Come Back Tomorrow'. Before she knew it everyone was gathering for the evening meal.

At the table Helen asked her, 'What are you doing tonight?'

Before she could answer, Buddy Phillips spoke up. 'She's going to Perkins' Cove with me.'

Helen's eyebrows lifted. 'You have your plans all made'

Jennifer smiled. 'Buddy says I ought to see the place.'

Sybil joined in, 'It's a fun place! There are a half-dozen artists' galleries and four or five night spots.'

The fat Randy Scott nodded. 'Helen and I are thinking of going over there to see what acts they have. Maybe we'll meet you.'

'Maybe,' Buddy said.

Helen gave Jennifer a questioning glance. 'That's all you have scheduled for tonight?'

'That's all,' she said, knowing that Helen was hinting about whether she might also be going to see Tim Moore.

Helen glanced at Sybil. 'What about you, princess?'

Sybil's pleasantly sullen face showed a smile. 'I'm seeing Jeff again. I don't know what he's planned yet. His folks are here this weekend from Boston and he wants me to meet them.'

'You're getting pretty tied up with this local yokel,' Helen said.

Sybil's cheeks flamed. 'He's not a local yokel. He's a teacher from Boston who spends his summers here with his folks. He's been down here getting their place ready. And I'm not tied up with him.'

'You're never with any of the company,' Helen told her.

Sybil said, 'Why should I be? Most of them are youngsters. At least two or three years younger than me.'

Randy Scott's round face showed a grin. 'Now we know the secret. You're too old for them!'

'You!' The brunette Sybil said in disgust as she got up from the table.

Helen and Jennifer finished dinner and left the table shortly afterwards. As they reached the hall Jennifer looked out the screen door and saw a familiar black foreign car drive up. It was Tim! Her heart gave a troubled leap.

The red-haired Helen showing a teasing look on her plain face. 'Someone to see you,' she said.

'Yes,' she agreed rather tautly. 'Will you excuse me a minute.' She left the other girl and went outside to the car, where Tim was seated behind the wheel.

The handsome leading man smiled up at her. 'I thought this might be a good time to catch you.'

'We've just finished in the dining-room,' she said.

'What about tonight?' Tim asked.

She hesitated. 'I've got plans,' she said finally.

Still smiling, he said, 'I hope they include me.'

'No,' she said, 'I'm afraid not. Do you mind?'

He lost his smile. 'Well,' he said, 'naturally I'm a little disappointed.'

'I'll see you any other night,' she said hastily.

'Sure,' he said.

'I'm sorry I have plans. But I made them earlier today.'

His face had brightened again. 'That's all right. Don't think anything about it. Have a nice evening. I'll be seeing you at the rehearsal tomorrow night.'

'Yes.'

'Are you giving that script of 'Come Back Tomorrow' some study in the meantime?' he asked.

'I've gone over it a lot. The part of Ann is wonderful.'

Tim said, 'I'm glad you agree.'

Just then Buddy Phillips came out of the house and, seeing Tim's car, came over to join them. The young man smiled at Tim and said, 'Roger Deering was trying to get in touch with you a while ago. He's at his cottage now. Maybe you ought to drive by.'

The leading man frowned. 'I will. Thanks. Have you any idea what he wants?'

'I think it's about the play at the end

of July,' Buddy said. 'The star he planned bringing in can't come and there may have to be a switch of plays.'

'I'll go over and talk to him,' Tim said. And to her, he added, 'See you tomorrow night.'

'Yes,' she said. As he drove off she turned to Buddy and asked him, 'Why did you come out? Were you afraid I'd break my promise to you?'

He laughed. 'I was a little nervous he might talk you out of it. And I did have that message for him.'

'What time are you planning to leave for Perkins' Cove?' she asked.

'No use going before nine,' he said. 'It's only after that it gets lively.'

'I'll be ready,' she said.

Perkins' Cove was a part of Ogunquit and the scene of a Greenwich Village type of stores, houses and night spots set amid lobster packing plants and weathered buildings holding art galleries. At night its lights gave it a glamour that was somewhat lacking in the daytime, though the ocean and the

146

boats docked on the river side offered a picturesque beauty at all times.

Buddy drove her over there shortly after nine and they found a dancing place overlooking the river and situated in the cellar of a restaurant which was very popular. A pianist and bass player offered pleasantly relaxed music for dancing or listening and they took a table from which they had a view of the spotlighted river and the boats docked just outside.

'I like it,' she told the young man.

'I thought you would,' Buddy said, looking pleased.

'How do you think the show is going to go?' she asked.

'If Donald Winter is as good as he was last night it will be great,' Buddy said. 'It was his best rehearsal.'

'I suppose the opening play is important.'

'Always. It sets the tone for the season.'

'Tim is playing the lead in the Noel Coward play, isn't he?' she said.

'Yes,' Buddy agreed. 'We've got the set painted now. And rehearsals will start Monday. Are you doing anything in it?'

'There's no part for me,' she said. 'But I'm trying out for a small part in the third play.'

'You mean 'Come Back Tomorrow',' he said. 'Ruth Crane is going to be the star in that. Roger Deering was going to have someone else come in and then he decided she was a big enough name for it.'

This was all news to Jennifer. She said, 'Well, she is a featured player in one of the big afternoon soap opera shows. So most people should know her.'

'That's what Roger thinks,' Buddy agreed. 'I hope you get the part you want.'

'Tim has promised to coach me in it. He was in the Broadway production,' she added proudly.

'I know,' Buddy said without sounding impressed.

They danced for a while and then

returned to their table to talk again. She asked him, 'Are you still determined not to work for your father when you leave here?'

'I am,' he said. 'I don't want to work for him until I can do a better job than anyone else. At this moment he can hire a dozen people to run his dinner-theatre shows better than me. I need more experience.'

'Won't he be angry with you?'

'I expect so,' Buddy said with a wry smile. 'But he'll get over it after a while.'

'In the meantime you could have a hard job finding work.'

'I know that, too,' he said. 'But it's the only way for me. I can't take on an executive post that is beyond me, even to please my father. If I started out in that phoney way there would just be no turning back. I'd have to go on bluffing. I'm not going to do it.'

She studied him seriously. 'You're full of ethics, aren't you?' she said. 'Always worried about some ethical problem,

149

your own or someone else's.'

'Are you going to fault me for that?'

'No. But it does make you a little different.'

'I prefer to be my own person,' Buddy told her. 'Having a rich father can make that difficult.'

'So it would seem,' she said.

She looked up from the table in time to see a couple coming down the stairway to the lounge. It was Tim Moore with Ruth Crane on his arm. They saw her at the same moment she recognised them. Fortunately there was a second room without dancing on the left and Tim saved an encounter between them by taking Ruth into that room. However, she was sure that Ruth had seen her and Buddy.

Buddy's back was to the stairs and he had missed seeing the newcomers. His pleasant face wore a questioning look. 'Something wrong?'

'Why do you ask?'

'You suddenly looked tense.'

'I don't think so,' she countered.

150

'You still look uneasy,' Buddy said.

'I'm tired,' she told him. 'I wish you'd take me home.'

He paid the check and they left. Fortunately Tim and Ruth had taken a table at the distant end of the other room so they did not see them as they made their way out of the downstairs lounge.

It was midnight by the time Buddy reached the boarding house. He said, 'I thought you were enjoying yourself and then suddenly you changed.'

'Not really,' she said. 'I just found myself a little tired. It was a good evening.' They were still seated in the front seat of his car.

'Honestly?'

'Yes.'

'Good enough to try it again some time?' he asked, worriedly.

She smiled. 'Why not?'

'After the rush of getting things started is over I'll remind you of that,' he promised.

'I won't mind,' she said.

He leaned over and kissed her. 'Maybe I was only guessing about it before. But I know now. I am in love with you, Jennifer.'

She touched his shoulder gently. 'It's the romantic setting!' she teased him. 'Remember your theory.'

'Forget my theories!' he said impatiently.

He escorted her inside and she went up to her room. This time she was the first home, neither Helen nor Sybil had returned yet. She wasn't sorry. It would give her a chance to get to bed before they came. Her mind was in a bothered state and the privacy was welcome.

After she was in bed she lay staring up at the ceiling through the darkness. Tim finding her and Buddy together in the dance place had given her quite a start. Not that she should mind. Hadn't Tim had Ruth Crane with him? But he had asked her out first and she'd refused. What would Tim think about her date with Buddy? How would he act when she met him next?

These questions and many more troubled her. She liked Buddy and enjoyed his company and he insisted he was in love with her. She couldn't say that she felt any strong romantic feelings for him, not in the way she did for Tim. There was something about the older man which touched her deeply. She knew it was wrong, but it was Tim she'd fallen in love with. And tonight she had deliberately hurt him!

8

Jennifer had dinner with Fred Short at the Shawmut Inn early Sunday evening. The dress rehearsal for 'No Sex Please, We're British' was scheduled for eight o'clock, so she presented herself at the summer hotel at six. Fred Short, immaculately dressed in a white summer suit, was waiting for her. They had a cocktail in the lounge and then went on to the elaborate, double-tiered dining-room overlooking the ocean.

When they were seated at a table near the window and had ordered, the alert Fred Short studied her from behind his horn-rimmed glasses. 'Are you happy at the playhouse?' he asked.

'It's wonderful,' she said enthusiastically.

'You and Tim Moore appear to be getting along well,' the hotel manager said a trifle too casually.

She felt her cheeks warm. 'Tim has been very kind to me.'

'He's an excellent actor,' Fred Short said. 'I'm sure he can help you a great deal with your work.'

'He already has,' she said. 'And he's going to try and get me a part in the play 'Come Back Tomorrow'. He was in the Broadway production.'

'I know,' Fred Short said. 'I saw it.' He paused. 'I feel a little responsible to your parents since they wrote and asked me to keep an eye on you for them.'

'Really, I'm not a child!' she protested.

'I know that,' he said. 'But you are young. Especially when compared to someone like Tim. I wouldn't like to see you become too interested in him.'

She pretended surprise. 'But we're merely good friends,' she protested.

'I would let it remain at that if I were you,' the hotel owner advised her.

Nothing more was said about Tim at dinner, but she knew that the alert Fred Short had delivered his message to her.

He had intended that she know he didn't approve of her close relationship with the older actor. She could understand his feelings, but at this point she didn't care to take the advice seriously. She knew that she was in love with Tim. All she was worrying about was how Tim would react to having seen her with Buddy Phillips the previous night.

When she had changed and reached the theatre she found it a madhouse of activity. Ken Chadwick, with Buddy's help, was seeing that the lighting, set and props were all exactly as they should be for the opening. Roger Deering was shouting orders from his seat in the auditorium and the actors were either in their dressing-rooms waiting to be called or fussing around backstage.

She found her prompt book and took a position in the wings down right. Randy was there, helping the electrician, and the show was to have its final rehearsal within a few minutes. She was waiting for the curtain to go up when Tim Moore came down to join her. He was dressed and made up for his role of the nervous young husband in the play. She could see how he'd skilfully applied make-up to his even features to make himself appear younger.

He smiled at her: 'Our minds must run in similar channels. I saw you at Perkins' Cove last night.'

'And I saw you.'

His eyes had a teasing glance in them. 'Buddy is a fine young man. And his father should be able to give him a great start since he has all those dinner-theatres.'

She said, 'He doesn't want to work for his father until he's gained more experience.'

Tim showed surprise. 'I wouldn't have expected that. But I'd say he's right.'

'I hope he is,' she said. 'His father is bound to be angry with him and he may find it hard getting work on his own.'

Tim said, 'I can tell you're interested in him and his future.'

She tried to hide her embarrassment. 'I like him,' she said awkwardly. 'And I thought it a good idea to go out with him. After the other night I was afraid we might be talked about.' It was an admission that she'd only gone out with Buddy to ease the situation for them. She hoped he'd understand and appreciate it.

His handsome face brightened. 'You're a wise little lady,' he said. Before he could say anything more Ken Chadwick shouted for them all to take their places as the curtain was going up.

The rehearsal was a complete success. And because everyone knew how much depended on the opening performance nearly all the company, including Tim Moore, went straight back to their lodging places to get a good night's rest. It was the same with the apprentice group, and Jennifer was grateful to be in bed early for a change.

The next day she worked in the box

office again. Roger Deering came to work there for a time as well. The theatre manager checked the tickets sold for the various performances and frowned slightly.

He said, 'We have a full opening night and a good Friday and Saturday, but the rest of the week is light and so is the Saturday matinee!'

Jennifer said, 'I suppose some of the summer people aren't here yet.'

'That's so,' he agreed. 'But a lot of them are. I think it has a lot to do with the opposition at Ogunquit. Shirley Booth is a strong name.'

'They have Walter Pidgeon in 'The Constant Husband' next week,' she said.

'And we have 'Blithe Spirit' with Tim Moore,' Roger Deering said, his actor's face clouding. 'Not exactly strong competition for a star like Pidgeon. How are the advance sales?'

'I haven't checked too closely,' she admitted.

'Let's do it now,' he said. And they

made an immediate check which did not produce a very hopeful picture. The sales for the second week were far below the comfortable gross already shaping up for week number one.

She said, 'We're about a third down so far.'

'Bad,' Roger Deering worried. 'We'll have to count on the new play the week after to make it up. Ruth Crane is starring in it and she's a television name. That means better box office.'

This incident worried her since it meant that Tim Moore was going to be starred in a play in which the week's business would be low. It was her first experience with the financial problems of the theatre world.

But she forgot all her concerns in the excitement of opening night. The parking lot was filled with cars twenty minutes before curtain time and Randy Scott and several of the other young male apprentices busied themselves guiding traffic with flashlights and setting up second lines of cars.

Roger Deering was dressed in black tie and tuxedo and the cast were all on edge. Star Donald Winter paced up and down uneasily by Jennifer before it was time to take his place on the other side of the stage.

'If I dry up in my lines shout them to me,' he warned her. 'If you don't I'll be in such a daze I won't even hear you.'

She promised that she'd give him any needed lines loudly and clearly. Then the house light were lowered and a hush came over the audience as the curtain went up. The magic that was theatre was now to begin. Jennifer hovered nervously in the wings following the play on the prompt script. It seemed to be going very well indeed.

Then suddenly, in a scene in which Donald Winter, Tim and Ruth Crane were on stage together, the British star went blank in his lines. Jennifer did exactly as he'd asked, giving him the line to get him started again in a fairly loud voice. It worked and the play went on smoothly to the end of the act. But she noticed as she gave the star his line Ruth Crane was gazing at her in anger. She thought no more of this as the play went on and the curtain lowered to a pleasant round of applause.

The curtain had barely fallen when Ruth Crane came across the stage to her and asked her angrily, 'What's the matter? Aren't you satisfied to prompt? Do you want to be seen and heard on the stage as well?'

Roger Deering had come around from out front and now he joined the angry actress and asked her, 'What is wrong?'

The attractive Ruth Crane turned to him and said, 'When she gave Donald his prompt she gave it so loud everyone in the house must have heard her. It broke the mood completely.'

The actor-manager looked unhappy. 'I did hear her,' he said. 'But I don't think it did any great harm.'

'It was amateurish and not needed!' Ruth said, still in a rage.

Roger Deering turned to Jennifer and

said, 'You shouldn't ever prompt that loudly.'

She felt she had to defend herself. 'Donald Winter asked me to give him his lines loudly. He was afraid he'd not hear otherwise.'

Tim Moore had come up by now and, hearing her, he agreed. 'I know Don made that request. And it worked. There was only a minute's delay. No harm was done!'

Ruth Crane gave him a sneering look. 'Amateur night!' she said with disgust and walked on to the dressing-room area.

Tim Moore watched her leave with an angry expression on his handsome face. 'She's suddenly very touchy!'

Roger Deering gave him a knowing look. 'You probably could figure it out if you tried.' Then he turned to Jennifer. 'I'd advise you to prompt less loudly, no matter what Donald Winter says.'

'Very well,' she said, feeling chastened for something for which she'd not been to blame.

Roger moved away to attend to something else and Tim remained with her for a moment. The leading man said, 'Don't worry about it, you did well.'

'There seems to be some difference of opinion,' she said ruefully.

'Pay no attention to Ruth,' Tim Moore said, and he also went back to his dressing-room to change his suit for the next act.

There were two other occasions during the performance when she had to supply lines to the star. She gave them in a voice pitched lower and managed to get them through to him. She was relieved when the curtain fell on the final act of the first night's performance.

The audience liked the play and Donald Winter and they were generous in their applause. She counted four curtain calls. Then it was over and everyone could relax.

Tim came to her quickly after the last of the curtain calls. 'You did fine,' he said. 'The cast is having a party at the Homestead. I'd like you to come.'

She shook her head. 'Not tonight, Tim. I wasn't in the play. Let's wait until the week I'm playing a part. Then I'll feel entitled to be there.'

He frowned. 'I'll be disappointed.'

'Better that than to have some others in the cast critical and angry,' she smiled up at him. 'You gave a fine performance. I'll see you tomorrow or some other night.'

'All right,' he said reluctantly. 'If that's what you think is best.' And he left her to change into his regular clothes.

It was shortly after that Buddy came and informed her, 'The apprentice company are having their own celebration. We're going to the Colony beach and have a bonfire. The Colony have given us permission. There will be lots of food and drink for everyone. You're invited.'

'Is everyone going?'

'Just about everyone,' he agreed.

'All right,' she said. 'Is there anything I can do to help?'

'Not a thing,' he told her. 'I'll take you in my car. We'll be leaving in about ten minutes.'

Buddy had a car full. Besides he and Jennifer there were Randy and Helen and the youth called Red. As they drove towards the beach Jennifer asked, 'Where's Sybil?'

'Off with her townie,' Helen said. 'I think that is getting serious. She's with him almost all the time.'

The bonfire was already started when they reached the beach. It was a pleasant, starry night and not too cold. The smell of the wood burning and the hot dogs filled the air with a tempting odour. Laughter and shouting went on around the big open blaze as one of the boys plied it with more logs.

Everyone squatted on the sand around the blazing fire and enjoyed its warmth and light. When Buddy arrived with his carload they were quickly accepted and found places at the fireside with the others.

Jennifer found herself seated between Buddy and the stout Randy. Randy bemoaned, 'I should be back rehearsing our act for tomorrow night.'

'Aren't you up in it yet?' she asked.

'Pretty well,' the fat young man said. 'But I want us to be in the best polished shape.'

Buddy leaned forward to speak to the fat man on the other side of Jennifer. He said, 'We're all planning to be there. So you'd better be good.'

Jennifer said, 'I thought the show went well tonight.'

Buddy spread his hands. 'Yes and no. Donald Winter isn't all that good. I saw the show with another star. He was better.'

'They got a good hand.'

'Bound to,' Buddy explained. 'There were a lot of the theatre backers there tonight. They always are enthusiastic. Wait until another night and you'll get a more honest reaction.'

'I suppose that's true,' she agreed.

Buddy said, 'I've been watching Roger Deering direct and I know that's what I want to do. I want to make directing my branch of theatre.'

She gave him an admiring look. 'I'm sure you'll make a good one.'

The young man with the unruly sandy hair said, 'The only trouble is, I have so much to learn.'

'As long as you know that and admit it, it shouldn't take all that much time,' she encouraged him.

He smiled. 'Thanks for making it sound easy. Even though I know it won't be.' And he asked, 'What about you?'

'I know more than ever I want to act.'

'And you're doomed to teach.'

'I'm going to do some acting this summer,' she said. 'And who knows, I may change my plans for the fall.'

His eyebrows lifted. 'Would your parents be happy about that?'

'You're not worrying about how your father is going to feel,' she pointed out.

'That's different.'

'I don't see how,' she said, studying his pleasant face in the reflection of the blazing bonfire.

'Hot dogs are ready!' somebody shouted.

There was a general reaction and a scrambling to the feet to join in the hot dog feast. She found herself paired with Helen. As they waited for Randy and Buddy to bring them soft drinks, the red-haired girl eyed her teasingly and said, 'I see you're not with Tim tonight.'

'No.'

'Why not?'

She shrugged. 'It's a cast party. I'd have felt out of place. And Ruth Crane is angry enough with me now.'

'Our leading lady really thinks Tim Moore is her property,' Helen agreed.

'They have been friends a long while,' Jennifer told the redhead.

'And now he can't see anyone but you!'

Jennifer felt embarrassed. 'That's an exaggeration.'

'Everyone is talking about it,' Helen said.

'He's anxious to help me with my acting.'

'I think he's interested in you as a person,' Helen said. 'You shouldn't try to deceive yourself about that.'

The boys returned with hot dogs and soft drinks and they all sat down again to eat. Jennifer felt relaxed and happy with the group. They were all mostly her own age or younger. It was an atmosphere she liked and understood. Yet she was just a little sad at missing being with Tim. She couldn't help thinking of him and what might be going on at the party at the Homestead.

Buddy suddenly stared at her and paused in biting off a piece of hot dog and bun to say, 'What's the matter, Jennifer? You seem a thousand miles away.'

'Sorry,' she apologised. 'I was thinking about the fun we're having here tonight. How wonderful it all is.'

'I doubt that,' the young man challenged her. 'I think your mind was on something else.'

The stout Randy picked this up. 'Sure,' he said. 'She's thinking of Tim Moore! Who else?'

Jennifer blushed and turned to him pleadingly. 'Randy, that isn't funny!'

'Sorry!' the stout man said at once. 'I guess that was a little out of line.'

'A lot out of line!' Helen told him. 'You'd better be funnier than that tomorrow night or we'll be cancelled before we start.'

A tall youth got up and began to strum a guitar, his lanky figure standing out against the glow of the blazing bonfire. He started singing a rock number and a lot of the others began to join in. Several couples jumped up to engage in a wild sort of dancing. The revelry was becoming increasingly loud.

She shouted to Buddy, 'I can't stand all this noise. I've got to get away from it for a little.'

'Okay,' he said, and he scrambled to his feet and helped her up.

They quickly strolled away from the boisterous scene and sought out a quiet stretch of beach. Here they could enjoy the wash of the waves and the tangy sea air. In the distance was the yellow glow of the bonfire and the echo of the banter and noisy music was subdued.

Buddy took her hand in his as they strolled along. 'The noise was getting pretty bad,' he said.

'It bothered me,' she told him.

'They always make too much racket,' Buddy worried. 'I hope the Colony people don't get angry. They were good enough to give us the beach.'

'They must have known the hazard,' she said. 'Probably it won't sound much worse at the hotel than it does here.'

'I hope not,' he said, glancing up towards the big hotel perched on its hill with most of its windows still lighted.

'I shouldn't have taken you away from the fun,' she said.

'No fun with you not along,' Buddy told her. 'I'd rather be with you than with them.'

They had walked as far as they could

without climbing some huge boulders to reach the other area of the beach. Now they stood and gazed out at the ocean reflecting the stars and showing the occasional lights of buoys and passing craft. She said, 'Well, we've started the season. I suppose before we know what is happening we'll come to the end.'

'The weeks will go by quickly,' Buddy agreed.

'Then we'll all part and go our different ways.'

'And probably a lot of the group won't ever see each other again.'

She turned to look at him in the darkness with a sad little smile. 'It's a melancholy thought! The friends we make are lost to us! So we have only the memories of the summer left.'

'Memories are better than nothing,' was Buddy's answer. 'I think most of us will learn a lot during the summer. We'll take that with us wherever we go along with our memories.'

'I suppose so,' she said.

Buddy turned to her. 'I know I'll remember you,' he said. 'Will you ever think about me?'

'I'll be bound to!'

He smiled at her. 'But it will be Tim Moore who'll have the majority of your thoughts.'

'How can you tell?'

'I know,' he said wryly. 'Anyhow, I'll just play along second best.'

'I can never think of you as that,' she protested.

'Thanks,' Buddy said, and he bent down slightly and kissed her on the lips. 'I suppose we'll have to go back or the'll be asking for us.'

'And gossiping about us!' she added.

'Yes,' he agreed. 'That too! But it has been fun having you here alone for a little.'

They strolled back to the bonfire where the merriment and music was still at a high. As they reached the spot where Helen and Randy were the red-haired girl spotted them and came across to join them.

At the first chance she took Jennifer aside and told her, 'Tim Moore came down here looking for you. He left his own party at the Homestead to find you here. When he learned you weren't here he left.'

9

Jennifer's prediction that the season would pass quickly proved to be all too true. Before she knew it the week's run of the first play ended. All the while they had been busily getting the second play rehearsed. She did manage to have a couple of dates with Tim Moore during this period. Once they went to a restaurant in Ogunquit after the evening performance and then one afternoon they went swimming at a quiet cove near the Shawmut Inn.

She worked with every department of the playhouse. It was exciting and she was gaining wonderful experience at the same time. Then came the morning of the tryouts for the third play in which Ruth Crane was starred and Jennifer was seeking the part of Ann.

In the several days before the tryouts Tim Moore gave her all his free time. It was only then that she discovered what a really excellent actor he was. He coached her in her lines and in the way she should move about the stage. Though the part was relatively short, he explained how it could be played to gain a lot of notice.

Roger Deering presided over the tryouts. Helen had been going to read for the part, but her act at the Jug Coffee Shop with Randy had turned into such a hit she no longer had interest in playing extra parts in the various plays. It was enough to be working before an audience every night after the performance. Thus Jennifer had no serious competition in seeking the role.

Still, Roger Deering was appreciative of the work she'd put into learning it when he heard her reading. From the dark auditorium he'd shouted, 'First rate, Jennifer. The part is yours and you'll be great in it.'

Ruth Crane, who was starring in 'Come Back Tomorrow', was less enthusiastic. The attractive professional actress turned to old character man R. Dudley Moffet, to say in a voice that everyone else could hear, 'If she speaks as loudly as she did when she was prompt girl, everyone is at least going to hear her.'

Jennifer felt her cheeks flaming, but she made no sign that she'd heard the older woman. She had satisfaction enough in seeing Ruth's chagrined expression when Tim came straight to her after the reading and said, 'You're going to get a round of applause of your own every night!'

Happily this turned out to be true. Jennifer fitted the minor role perfectly. She worked harder than she ever had before since she wanted Tim Moore to be proud of her. As a result she did get a special mention in all the reviews and the audience loved her and reserved a special ovation for her.

Roger Deering came to her after the opening night of the play and said, 'I'm delighted with what you've done with the part.'

'Tim helped me.'

'I'm sure he must have,' the owner of the company agreed. 'Be that as it may, I'm going to find you some other good roles in the plays which I'll be selecting for the balance of the season.'

Even Buddy came to her and professed his admiration of the way she'd played the part. 'You were great,' he said.

'Thanks!' she said, the applause still in her ears.

Tim Moore was ecstatic about the way she played the part. But everyone expected this of him, in a way Jennifer knew she was his creation. He had seen her possibilities in the role and coached her perfectly. Ruth Crane treated her coldly and didn't congratulate her. In the one scene in which they played together Ruth made it as difficult as possible for her.

But Jennifer was not to be discouraged. Her parents were coming for the weekend to see her in the role and hotel manager Fred Short was one of the first to come and praise her at the party held at the Shawmut Inn this time.

'I'm proud to be your foster-uncle, Jennifer,' he said, joking about the relationship. 'Everyone was talking about you between the acts.'

'Tim made it possible,' she said simply.

'Did he?' Fred Short said, sounding a little worried at this. 'Well, no matter who helped it was you who gave the fine performance.'

When the opening night party was at its height she and Tim slipped out on the veranda of the Shawmut. It was warm now and more pleasant out there than in the crowded room where everyone was dancing.

The first thing Tim did was embrace her and then hold her a little distance away from him proudly. 'You made this a night I'll never forget,' he promised her.

'Nor will I,' she said a little breathlessly.

'There are no doubts in my mind now,' he said. 'You can act.'

'Because you've believed in me.'

'I have,' he agreed. 'But that is only part of it.'

'My parents are coming to see me,' she said, her eyes shining. 'I want you to meet them.'

Tim looked a little uneasy. 'I'll be glad to,' he said. 'But how are they going to feel about me?'

'They'll like you! Why shouldn't they?'

The handsome leading man turned away and stared out at the ocean. 'I've been seeing a lot of you. I have an idea they won't exactly be happy about that.'

'I'm twenty-one!' she said firmly.

'So you are,' he smiled. 'But that still won't have any bearing on whether they approve or not.'

'I'm old enough to make my own decisions!'

'Parents rarely ever think that about an only daughter,' the actor said.

'I don't care what they say,' Jennifer

told him. 'I was never happier in my life. And the one most responsible for it is you.'

He put an arm around her. 'Thank you, Jennifer,' he said in a tender voice. 'My being with you has been like a renewal of life. Everything that seemed so stale is suddenly fresh again. I was beginning to hate the playhouse. It's my tenth year here, you know. But you've changed it for me.'

She frowned slightly. 'Why should you hate it?'

'Because it's the mark of my failure in a sense,' he said. 'Just as it is now the scene of your success. If I were really a success in the theatre I wouldn't be returning here, year after year. By now I'd be heading a touring package show or having some big hit in the theatre or in films.'

His explanation worried her. She suddenly realised that it was true. She said, 'But you deserve success, you are such a fine actor.'

Tim said, 'You'll find that you need

to be more than capable in the theatre. You need to be lucky.'

'Then you will be lucky one day,' she said. 'You deserve it.'

He smiled at her. 'Let's hope so. But it will have to come soon. I've got a lot less time than you, I'm afraid.'

'Don't talk that way! You'll spoil the night for me!' she said, pleading.

He touched his lips to the crown of her hair. 'I'm sorry. I was being selfish. This is your night! That's all that matters. And somehow I'll manage to get along with your parents.'

'There won't be any trouble,' she promised.

The door from the lounge opened and Fred Short came out. He surveyed them from the open door with the music loud behind him as the dancing and celebrating went on. He shut the door and then came out to them.

He said, 'You two have found the most romantic spot.'

Tim laughed. 'I'd like to think so.'

'I was weary from the talk and

music,' Jennifer explained.

A knowing smile crossed Fred Short's usually serious face. The eyes behind the glasses were fixed on her. 'I understand,' he said quietly, as if he did thoroughly understand.

'My parents are coming down Friday,' she said.

'I know,' Fred Short said. 'I have a room for them.'

'I hope they'll like me,' she said.

'Why not? Everyone else agrees you are perfect in the part,' he said.

'And I want them to meet Tim,' she said, wanting to get the hotel manager's reaction.

His reaction was a curiously wary one. He said, 'Yes, they will surely want to know Tim.' Then he told her, 'I came out to see if you'd dance with me.'

'Of course,' she said, not wanting to leave Tim but unable to refuse the hotel manager's request. It was a neat ploy on his part to get them back inside with the others.

The crisis came for her when her

parents arrived. They came to the play on Friday night and they were so enthusiastic they wanted to attend again Saturday evening. She and Tim had the matinee to do, but she arranged to have him meet her parents at an early lunch at the Shawmut.

The lunch was set for twelve. She drove over to the hotel early in her own car as she didn't want Tim to be under her parents' scrutiny any longer than possible. In this way she was able to have some time with them alone before he joined them for the luncheon.

She met her parents on the veranda of the chalet room in which they were staying. Since it was a nice day they could sit in the open and watch the ocean while they chatted. Her father, Emery Bruce, was a successful insurance man, only about a year or two older than Tim Moore, though he was greying and a bit overweight so that he seemed much more mature. Her mother, Lucy, had the same fine features as Jennifer and had kept her slender figure, but her hair was darker in shade and there were tiny wrinkle lines at her eyes and around her mouth to betray her age. Both parents were fairly worldly and usually generous people in their estimate of others.

As Jennifer sat chatting with them, her father abruptly said, 'I understand you've dated this Tim Moore a lot.'

'He's been wonderful to me, Father,' she said. 'I owe my success in the part to his coaching.'

'But it's your talent,' her mother demurred.

Her father had a steely glint in his grey eyes. 'I hope he hasn't taken advantage of your romantic feelings about the theatre to force himself on you.'

Her eyes widened in dismay. 'Tim isn't that sort of man, Father.'

'Your father is only trying to protect you,' her mother said. 'There has been some talk. Fred felt it his duty to tell us.'

186

She frowned. 'I don't know what talk you've heard. But I don't think what Tim and I have between us is the business of anyone else.'

Emery Bruce cleared his throat. 'I know he looks young on the stage, but I hear he is older than me.'

'You're not so old!' Jennifer protested.

'It is not a matter of my being old,' her father said. 'It is just that from a romantic angle a man of my age is bound to be old for you.'

'That's right, darling,' her mother said. 'You must think carefully about this romance with Tim Moore. I understand there are several nice boys in the company who are fond of you. If you want dates, why don't you date them?'

'Because I happen to prefer Tim's company,' she said unhappily. 'Isn't that of some importance?'

'He's older and more sophisticated,' her father agreed. 'That doesn't mean he is ideal company for you. Your mother and I aren't asking you to break your friendship with him. We only ask that you keep it within bounds. I don't want to wake up some morning and find myself with an actor son-in-law two or three years older than me. Give your mother and I some consideration!'

Jennifer exclaimed, 'Shouldn't I be considered first?'

'We are considering you,' her mother said placatingly. 'Not only is this man older than you, but he is not well-off in a financial way.'

'He's an excellent actor!' Jennifer said.

'Which doesn't mean he ever has to be a good earner,' her father said. 'It would be criminal for you to marry an older man who couldn't provide properly for you.'

'I'm not worried about that,' she said.

'I am,' Emery Bruce replied firmly. 'Fred Short tells me this Tim Moore may not even have his summer's work here next year.'

She gasped. 'Why not? He's been

leading man here for ten years! Surely you aren't going to have him let go because he's shown an interest in me?'

'Not at all,' her father said. 'You should know better than that.'

Her mother said, 'Your father is not that sort of person.'

'I don't know what to think,' Jennifer told them. 'Not after listening to all this. Why shouldn't Tim Moore return here another season?'

'Because he'll be a year older for one thing,' her father said. 'There is such a thing as age limit even in summer stock leading men.'

'He doesn't look old!'

Her mother pointed out, 'But, dear, he's been here so long. Many people may have tired of seeing him in play after play.'

'That is the main gist of it,' her father said. 'Fred Short is a member of the theatre board and he says Roger Deering plans to change policy next season. Instead of producing plays here he'll book packaged productions with a star the same as Ogunquit. In this way the theatre here will be able to compete with the Ogunquit Playhouse more successfully.'

Jennifer was stunned. 'I don't believe it. There has been nothing said about it among the company.'

'It isn't completely settled yet,' her father said. 'But Fred is sure it will be. Roger claims the theatre has been making less money than last year. The gross receipts have been declining each year. There is no other answer.'

She refused to accept it. She said, 'I'll believe it when it's official.'

'Believe what you like,' her father said. 'I only want you to know the facts. Tim Moore will no longer be a star when the change takes place. He'll be lucky to find a job next summer. Unless he takes work in a touring package.'

Jennifer was suddenly afraid for Tim. She asked her father, 'Please don't say any of this to him, will you?'

'No,' he said. 'As a matter of fact I promised Fred Short only to tell you.

They don't want rumours flying around too early.'

She felt a small relief. 'If it is true, I don't want Tim to know until he has to. It will be a blow to him.'

Her mother and father exchanged looks. Then her mother said, 'You are very protective of him, dear.'

'I think I'm in love with him,' she said simply.

Her father scowled. 'We've been afraid you'd say something like that.'

'Don't rush into this recklessly, darling,' her mother pleaded. 'You have your school to teach in the autumn. Use that time to think this all out clearly. When you are away from the theatre and these summer surroundings which glamourise everything.'

'Mother, I'm not sure I want to teach high school dramatics in the fall,' she said. 'I may try to get some regular theatre work.'

'Oh, no!' her mother said, crestfallen.

Her father continued to look stern. 'I can see that Fred didn't exaggerate this at all. This Tim Moore has swept you off your feet. I've always felt you to be a fairly level-headed girl.'

'You don't understand,' she worried. 'You have no idea how deep this thing is between Tim and me. We fill needs for each other. No matter what the difference in our ages, I know we could be happy together.'

Emery Bruce listened to this in silence. Then he said, 'Has this fellow asked you to marry him?'

'No.'

'Do you think he will?' her father wanted to know.

'I hope he will,' she said sincerely.

'Jennifer,' her mother lamented.

Her father made a motion for her mother to be silent as he said, 'I hope he will ask you to marry him, too. This may surprise you, but I hope it because it will prove he does care for you and that you're not merely a passing amusement with him!'

'Father!' she exclaimed.

'Such things are known to be,' her

father said. 'So let us give him the benefit of the doubt and assume that he is going to propose to you. I am sure he won't come to your mother and me for permission. He'll make his offer to you. When he does, I want you to give it the greatest consideration. Think of all that we've told you. Don't blind yourself to the facts. Take care before you commit yourself to him.'

'I agree, Father,' she said soberly. 'In return I ask that you and Mother be pleasant to him and try to understand him.'

'Of course we'll be pleasant to him,' her mother declared.

'Father?' Jennifer asked him.

He sighed. 'It's going to take some effort, but I'll try and treat him like an old friend of the family. But don't you think it changes anything. You know how we feel.'

It was fortunate that they had finally reached this settlement as at that very moment Tim Moore was driving his big black sports car into the parking lot.

She went down to meet him and show him to her parents' veranda. She tried to forget all that had been said and present a happy face for the man she loved.

Tim stepped out of his car in smart sports clothes, looking strangely timid for him. 'Are you ready to feed me to the lions?' he asked.

She managed a smile. 'I've taken the edge off their appetites. You'll be fairly safe.'

He stared at her. 'They must have been tough. You look weary.'

She grimaced. 'Entertaining parents is never an easy task. Come along.'

It was understandable that there should have been a certain tenseness about the meeting. But, all in all, Jennifer felt that the luncheon went very well. Her mother was polite if restrained and her father didn't glare at Tim more than once. They had the excuse of the matinee to get them away as soon as the meal was over. They said their goodbyes and walked out to the parking lot to get their cars.

Tim hesitated a moment with her as soon as they were alone. He said, 'I don't think they approve of me.'

She laughed ruefully. 'No one was ever good enough for their daughter.'

Tim regarded her tenderly. 'I'd feel exactly the same way. I don't blame them.'

'Don't play the paternal role with me. It isn't becoming,' she warned him.

'Sorry,' he said. 'I forgot about that.' He glanced at his wristwatch. 'We have to hurry. It will soon be curtain time.'

'I'll see you at the theatre,' she promised.

Each headed for their car and then drove out of the Shawmut parking lot in the direction of the theatre. Now that she was alone Jennifer thought about some of the things which her parents had said and which were now bothering her. The news that the policy of the theatre might change had been particularly worrisome. So many jobs of people whom she liked would be eliminated.

Worst of all, it would mean an end of Tim's starring seasons at the playhouse.

The matinee audience was already gathering as she drove around to the rear and parked by the big yellow house where she and the other apprentices lived. She then locked her car and hurried across to the stage door. R. Dudley Moffet was finding his way up the steps with difficulty.

'Good afternoon, Mr Moffet,' she greeted him as she helped him up the stairs. 'You're almost as late as I am.'

'But I don't appear until the second act,' the old man said in his courtly fashion. 'So I don't need to be here so early. By the way, I'm amazed by the fine acting job you're doing as Ann. You're giving the role the style of a seasoned actress.'

'Thank you,' she said as they entered the backstage area and parted.

Because the cast of 'Come Back Tomorrow' was small, she had her own dressing-room. As she sat making up before the large mirror over the counter on which her make-up material was set out, she continued to worry about the contemplated change of policy at the playhouse. R. Dudley Moffet, whom she'd just assisted up the stairs, was another of the actors who would find difficulty getting other summer employment. He was almost totally blind, but Roger Deering allowed him extra rehearsal time to compensate for this. It was unlikely he'd get this treatment anywhere else.

10

The long, bright days of July began to give way to the shorter ones of August. The July Fourth Independence Day holiday was ancient history and people were now discussing Labour Day Weekend and whether the holiday would be pleasant. The nights came earlier and were perceptibly chillier. While the summer season at Kennebunkport was still in full surge it would only be a short while until the tide of tourists ebbed and end-of-the-season sales signs appeared in the store windows.

The playhouse was half-way through its season and the balance of the plays had all been chosen. Ruth Crane was starring in 'Forty Carts' as August began. This was to be followed by 'Dial M for Murder', with Tim Moore playing the lead, then 'Six Rooms With

View', in which Ruth Crane was to star again, and the final play of the year, 'Prisoner of Second Avenue', with Tim the featured name. It had been evenly divided.

Life had settled down to a kind of routine among the company. After the departure of her parents Jennifer had no more comments from hotel owner Fred Short about her romance with Tim. Nor did Roger Deering say anything. But she'd heard some sarcastic comments which a vindictive Ruth Crane had uttered. The attractive leading woman couldn't stand the thought of losing Tim to someone younger.

Randy Scott and Helen had become the rage of the village. Their show in the coffee house had become a 'must' for tourists all over the region. Each night after the show they gave a performance in the second-floor coffee house at Dock Square and each night the cramped area was filled with the parked cars of visitors. There were rumours that a Boston hotel wanted to hire the two for the fall and winter season. Two-Ton had triumphed with his idea.

Other exciting news was the engagement of the curvaceous Sybil to Jeff Martin. It turned out that Jeff was the only son of a wealthy Boston family and this would mean that Sybil would not be pursuing her theatrical career.

The stout Randy summed it up best when he said, 'Considering the career, she's better off without it!'

Roger Deering had not made any public announcement yet about the season for next year, but it was generally known that business at the red barn playhouse had been spotty. One night the crowd would be excellent and the next the house would be half-empty. Jennifer felt positive the new policy would be stated during the final week of the season.

During the run of 'Forty Carats', stage manager Ken Chadwick's wife became ill and he had to leave the playhouse and go to her in New Jersey.

This left Buddy Phillips in full charge of the backstage activities. The sandy-haired young man proved himself in this capacity and mounted the production of 'Dial M For Murder' completely on his own.

Jennifer had become the apprentice most featured as an actress during the season. Her appearance in 'Come Back Tomorrow' had made her a favourite of the company with local playgoers and they encouraged her every appearance. They seemed to think that she was their special discovery. And in a way she was.

The constant playing of new parts was giving her valuable experience. Tim continued to coach her and she felt more in command of her acting technique than ever before. Though she continued to see a great deal of Tim Moore, she still occasionally went off with the apprentice group for parties, or saw Buddy Phillips alone.

One night during the week when they were playing 'Dial M For Murder' and rehearsing 'Six Rooms With View'

Buddy invited her to Poor Richard's Tavern on the main road to Ogunquit. She had heard that the orchestra there was very good, but she'd never been there. Tim had been asked to have drinks with a summer family after the show so she was left on her own. Because of this she took Buddy up on his invitation.

Buddy drove her over to Poor Richard's in his car. On the way he asked her, 'Have you made your mind up yet what you are going to do at the end of the season?'

'I'm not sure,' she admitted, sitting back against the leather seat of his small sports car.

His eyes on the road, Buddy said, 'You haven't much time left to decide.'

'I know.'

'Labour Day is coming quickly.'

'I know,' she sighed in the semi-darkness of the car's front seat. 'And it seems only yesterday that we were all arriving here to start the season.'

'That's the way it always is,' he

agreed. 'I can honestly say I've learned a lot. And the hard way. These last few weeks have been terrific with Ken not here.'

'You've managed beautifully.'

'I've squeezed by.'

She gave him a smiling glance. 'What about your fall and winter plans? Have you changed your mind about running your father's dinner-theatres?'

'No. He sent one of his main men down here to talk to me last week,' Buddy said. 'But I told him I wasn't interested.'

'Isn't he puzzled by that?' she asked.

'My father never gets puzzled,' Buddy said wryly. 'He flies into a rage when you don't do what he expects. But this time he can be in a rage.'

'And you?'

'I'm going to New York. Ken has given me some names. He thinks I might get a stage management job in one of the television studios.'

'That would be good.'

'It would be a start and I might do

some off-Broadway things on the side,' Buddy said.

She was impressed by the young man's determination to be independent and to learn his trade. Buddy was, apart from stout Randy Scott, the most dedicated of all the apprentice members of the playhouse group.

They reached Poor Richard's and gave the car to an attendant. Inside a duo composed of an organist and a drummer were offering some loud rock music. A polite captain found them tables in a remote corner of the big room, far away from the music. While it wasn't exactly quiet it was better for conversation than almost any other spot. The floor in the centre of the room was filled with dancers of all sorts.

Buddy smiled at her as they sat at the table. 'I hope you don't mind this.'

'It's another rock spot,' she said. 'But we're far enough away to manage.'

After they ordered he invited her to dance. The orchestra just happened to be playing a pleasant popular ballad so they managed well and the floor wasn't too crowded. When the duo began to offer rock again they hastily went back to their table.

Buddy smiled at her as they sat at the table together. 'I heard your name mentioned today.'

'Did you?'

'Yes. Roger was lamenting that he didn't have a part for you in the final show. But he said you'd be understudying Ruth Crane in any case.'

'I'm understudying her now,' she said. 'And I'm doing the Puerto Rican woman as well. It's only a bit part. But at least it gets me on stage.'

'Which is where you belong.'

'I'm glad you think so,' she said.

'Everyone agrees,' he told her.

'I'm sorry to see the season end,' Jennifer said.

'So am I,' the young man agreed. 'It means making a lot of decisions. And from what I hear, Roger Deering is saying this is going to be the last regular season. The theatre is booking package shows next year.'

She was at once interested. 'I've heard that. Do you think it's true?'

'Yes,' Buddy said. 'Ogunquit has package shows and they are crowded all the time. Roger knows the playhouse needs stars.'

'So the regular won't be coming back next year?'

'None of the actors,' he agreed. 'Ken Chadwick will be here. They have to have a stage manager and I've been offered the post of assistant. If nothing better comes up I'll take it.'

'It's too bad,' she said. 'I hate to see the playhouse change. It won't be the same.'

'Hard for the actors. Especially Tim and Ruth. Not to mention poor old blind R. Dudley Moffet.'

'He soon ought to retire.'

Buddy nodded. 'Maybe he will. But I have an idea that might work out.'

'What?'

'I don't see any reason why the

206

playhouse couldn't keep on having an apprentice group. Roger Deering depends on the ones here now to do a lot of the rough work and to usher and help in the box office. Once he does away with the apprentices he will have to hire regular help for all those chores. And even if he hires local youngsters, it will cost money and they won't have the same interest in the theatre.'

'So?'

Buddy was enthusiastic as he went on, 'I say, have an apprentice group. Let them do the extra work around the theatre as they always have. And also have acting classes for them and let them watch the package rehearsals and performances. Then on Sunday nights when the theatre is dark let them present a weekly play.'

She saw how excellent the idea was and said, 'I think that would be a wonderful idea. But you'd need people to train the apprentices.'

'Easy,' he said. 'Hire someone like R. Dudley Moffet to train them in speech and diction, even a blind man can do that, have you act as a sort of assistant director, and let Roger Deering put the final polish on the performances. Ken Chadwick and I would look after backstage as usual.'

'I don't know whether I have experience enough,' she demurred.

'You have planned to teach in high school,' he reminded her. 'These youngsters will be mostly of that age with a few older. Of course you could do it.'

'I'd try if Roger Deering is interested,' she said. 'It would keep the theatre alive as a producing unit in a sort of way.'

'Exactly how I feel,' Buddy said. 'So maybe the change of policy needn't work out too badly.'

'I see one flaw.'

'What?'

'There's nothing in your plan for Tim Moore?'

'Sorry,' he said with a teasing smile. 'Wouldn't you expect me to want to eliminate him? Then I might have a chance with you.'

She smiled in return. 'I'm serious, though. What is going to happen to Tim?'

The young man shrugged. 'No place for him in the set-up I've outlined. He doesn't like to direct.'

'I worry about him.'

'If he's as good as he's supposed to be,' Buddy said. 'I think he'll find something. We both know he is a competent actor and he could easily change to directing if he wanted to.'

'It would seem a waste,' she said. 'He makes a handsome figure on-stage.'

'But he's getting older every year. He'd be better off to begin directing. Character men don't earn nearly that much. And in a year or two those are the parts he'll be forced to play.'

She sighed wistfully. 'I never used to think about age, except to be impatient to be older. Now I wish I could somehow hold the calendar back.

'A lot of people feel that way,' Buddy

said. 'The smart ones plan ahead. Roger Deering used to be a leading man. But he was getting older and so he bought the playhouse. He can stay there for ever as long as he makes it pay. Tim needs something like that.'

'I must talk to him,' she decided.

Her chance came a few days later when she and the leading man went swimming after an early afternoon rehearsal. Because Tim had struck up a friendship with the young manager of the Colony they had been going to the Colony pool. Now that the season was waning the pool was not all that busy.

They found deck chairs at the far left end away from most of the people and stretched out there in the sun after their swim. It was a lazy August day with no clouds in the sky and she called on all her resources of confidence as she leaned up on an elbow and addressed herself to him.

She said, 'Tim, have you ever thought of your plans for the future?'

The handsome Tim turned to her

and removed his sun glasses to eye her quizzically. 'May I ask what brought this on?'

Jennifer said, 'You haven't answered me!'

'Of course I haven't answered you,' Tim Moore said. 'What I want to know is why you'd ask such a question? I'm an actor. So I act! What more planning can I do?'

'You might find you aren't wanted as an actor one day.'

'Aha!' he said. 'I think I have it. You've been hearing the rumours that Roger is changing the playhouse policy.'

'Well?'

'He's talked about it for years but he's never done it,' Tim argued. 'I know Roger. He enjoys directing. When it comes to the concrete business of planning the season he'll change his mind and have a resident company.'

'Maybe not this time.'

'I say, yes.'

'But suppose he doesn't?' she worried.

'Suppose he does change to package deals?'

Tim's handsome face shadowed. 'Then I'll simply have to find work somewhere else. There must be plenty of other places with resident companies.'

'Not all that many from what I hear.'

'Are you trying to discourage me?' Tim asked.

'No. I want you to be realistic. With your experience you should turn to production or direction. Some sort of executive position.'

Tim stared at her. 'I've never liked the idea of directing.'

'After the way you coached me I know you've a genius for it.'

'That's different,' he objected.

'Not really,' she said. 'I wish you weren't so stubborn.'

Tim laughed and reached over and took her hand. 'And I wish you weren't so young and worried.'

'I'm thinking of you,' she said. 'Of us, if you like.'

He was studying her with fond eyes. 'If anyone is going to worry, let it be me. Will you?'

'I might just as well not talk to you,' she sighed. 'You never listen to me anyway.'

And it was true. For all that he insisted he was in love with her the older actor treated her like a child when it came to her making any constructive suggestions.

The night 'Six Rooms With View' opened it was unusually hot and sultry. The nights had been cooler and this was a throwback to early in the season. The house was filled and the play was well received. Ruth Crane and Tim Moore, as the two people who meet and have a brief romantic fling in an empty apartment while out apartment hunting, made a great impression on the audience. Ruth was at her best, though she'd been miserable to Jennifer all during rehearsals.

Jennifer was playing a bit part and understudying Ruth. In turn, Helen was understudying Jennifer. Since the part was of only three or four speeches and one entrance there was no great problem in that. At the same time Helen and Randy kept busy with their coffee house comedy show.

Roger Deering was having a yearly party for the cast at the Colony Lounge that night after the show. Everyone was excited about this and Roger had made an exception and invited a few of the apprentices who were helping with that particular production.

Tim drove her to the Colony after the performance and they went in and seated themselves at the outside tables which had been reserved for them. Soon the others began arriving and taking their places. Ruth Crane came with Roger Deering. She was wearing a smart white halter-type dress and looked stunning. Buddy Phillips was also there on his own.

Drinks were served and conversation grew more lively around the table. Seated by Tim, she was conscious of angry stares from Ruth. She tried to avoid looking her way and talked to Ken Chadwick, who was on her other side. The evening went on and Jennifer began to wish she was anywhere else but at the party. Ruth, across the table, was making taunting remarks which she could hear. Tim and Roger Deering had wandered off somewhere and Jennifer felt very much alone.

All at once Ruth, who seemed to have been drinking heavily, got to her feet and came unevenly over to her. The face of the attractive older actress was crimson and she leered down at Jennifer.

'I want to talk to you,' she said.

Jennifer glanced up at her. 'Well?'

'I don't want to talk here,' the actress said impatiently. 'Come out by the pool.'

'I don't think we have anything to discuss!'

Ruth smiled drunkenly. 'That's where you're wrong. We have plenty to discuss. We should have done it long ago.'

Jennifer realised that some of the others were listening now and she didn't want a scene to be made. She thought too much of Roger to want to have his party spoiled. She looked around and saw that Roger and Tim were standing by the bar talking earnestly about something. She didn't want to interrupt what might be an important business talk, so she decided to humour the drunken Ruth.

Getting up, she said, 'All right. Let's go.'

Ruth led the way and they walked out to the patio which surrounded the lighted pool. It was very pleasant out there on this warm night. As soon as they were alone out there Ruth turned on her angrily and said, 'Why are you trying to destroy Tim?'

Jennifer said, 'I don't know what you mean!'

'Your childish flirtation with him is costing him his future,' Ruth told her.

'I can't see that!' Jennifer protested.

'Tim and I were in love until you

216

came along,' Ruth told her.

She knew this wasn't so. She had heard from Tim that while he respected Ruth as an actress, he thought her a very difficult person to get along with. He'd been friendly with her, but had never considered her seriously.

She said, 'I don't think that's true. Tim was never in love with you. You may have been in love with him. If so, I'm sorry.'

'Thank you for being sorry,' Ruth said with venom in her tone. 'I really appreciate that.'

'I mean it,' she said. 'I don't want to cause anyone unhappiness.'

'Then you should give up Tim.'

'Why?'

'You're making him ridiculous,' Ruth told her, her voice slurring over the words. 'If he'd married me I could have found him work in my television show. And I know people who would do things for him.'

'If you can help him I should think you'd do it anyway,' she said. 'I'm sure he'd help you in any way he could.'

Ruth laughed harshly. 'Help him? Why should I help him to have a life with you? You're nothing but a little upstart he's coached as he'd coach a parrot! You couldn't do anything on your own!'

'I'm the first to admit he's helped me!' she said.

Ruth sneered at her. 'Miss Mealy-Mouth, with your precious sentiments. You don't fool me!'

'I think you should talk directly to Tim if you think you have anything to say to him,' Jennifer told her. 'I was right in the first place. We haven't anything to say to each other!' And she turned to leave.

'I'll teach you! You little cheat!' Ruth said in a rage. And she grabbed hold of a surprised Jennifer's arm and dragged her back. Then she swung her and sent her hurtling into the pool!

11

Jennifer had been taken completely by surprise. In the few seconds between when Ruth Crane grabbed her and she was sent spinning into the cold pool she had no chance to collect her thoughts and protect herself. The descent into the water was less dangerous than it was humiliating. She quickly got to her feet and stood up, forlorn, dripping and angry, while Ruth laughed drunkenly.

The first person to be aware that something was wrong and arrive on the scene was Buddy Phillips. The young man took in the situation with one look. He gave the inebriated Ruth and angry glance and went to the pool to assist Jennifer up the steps.

Ruth hooted, 'I showed you! Now I'm leaving!' And she turned to go inside.

Jennifer quickly told Buddy, 'Go with

her! She's driving alone and she is in no fit state to be behind the wheel!'

'What about you?' Buddy worried.

'I'll make out,' she said. 'I'll go in the side door to the ladies' room and fix up a little, then I'll have Tim drive me home.'

Buddy was watching Ruth's departing figure. 'Of all the stupid tricks!' he said with disgust.

She gave him a push. 'Go on! Hurry! Otherwise she'll be in her car and driving before you get to her.'

He started and called over his shoulder, 'Do you want me to speak to Tim?'

'No. Just hurry after her! I'll manage,' she said.

Buddy went inside in pursuit of the drunken actress. Thoroughly drenched, she took the concrete walk alongside the hotel and made her way to the ladies' room in the corridor leading to the lounge by a roundabout route. She quickly took off her dress and wrung it out. Then she put it on again and fixed her wet hair as best she could. Ruth had certainly made a mess of her, she thought grimly.

She also thought how unreasonable the other girl's comments and accusations had been. When she fixed herself up as well as she could she went down the corridor to the lounge where the party was progressing without anyone having really noticed that the bizarre scene had taken place by the pool. Tim had moved away from the bar and was standing talking to R. Dudley Moffet close to the door, so she had no difficulty getting his attention.

He came out and stared at her in disbelief. 'What in the world happened to you?' he wanted to know.

She smiled wryly. 'Ruth shoved me in the pool. I should have been on my guard.'

'She did what?'

'Threw me in the pool.'

'Where is she?' Tim asked, looking around wrathfully.

'She left. I sent Buddy after her. She

wasn't fit to drive her car. I hope he was able to persuade her to let him take the wheel.'

'I doubt it,' Tim said grimly. 'She becomes crazy when she drinks too much. Tonight she seems to have outdone herself.'

Roger Deering joined them and gave her a surprised look. 'How did you get all wet?' he wanted to know. She quickly told him.

Tim was angry. 'Ruth has to be punished for this. She could have seriously hurt Jennifer.'

Roger Dering said, 'It was a crazy thing for her to do. I'll talk to her.'

'I don't want to cause any trouble,' she said. 'After all, she was drinking.'

'No excuse,' Tim said bitterly. 'She's been wanting to get at you.'

'I agree,' Roger Deering said, his actor's face showing a troubled expression. 'She must be given a strong lecture.'

'At the very least,' Tim said. 'I'd better get you back to the boarding house before you catch pneumonia.'

'I would like to get out of these wet things,' she agreed.

They said goodnight to Roger Deering and then hurried out to Tim's car. As he headed it out on to the road, he said, 'I wonder how Buddy made out with her.'

Jennifer said, 'I hope she let him drive.'

They drove along the same route by the river which Ruth had to follow earlier. As they neared the Dock Square area Jennifer saw the blinking light of a police car ahead of them and a lot of other cars stopped. Her throat tightened as she at once suspected there had been an accident with Ruth responsible.

At the wheel Tim was frowning as he stared ahead. 'What is going on?' he wondered as he slowed the car to a halt.

They got out and ran ahead in time to see stretchers being placed in an ambulance. There had been a two-car collision — one car had hit the other side on. Jennifer surveyed the wreck and in a sickening moment recognised one of the wrecked cars as Ruth's.

She ran ahead to the State Trooper supervising operations and in a pleading voice asked him, 'Tell me who was hurt?'

The young police officer gave her a sharp look. 'You're from the theatre company, aren't you?'

'Yes. I'm sure a friend of mine was in one of the cars!'

He looked grim. 'There were theatre people in the car that caused the accident. A young woman at the wheel and a man with her.'

'Were they hurt badly?'

'Badly enough,' the State Trooper said. 'They've just taken them to Biddeford Hospital by ambulance. The four people in the other car have also been taken there in a police car. They're not as badly hurt.'

Tim came up. 'What happened?' he asked her.

She quickly told him. She was tearful

now. 'I should never have sent Buddy along with her. She's refused to let him drive and he's gone along anyway. Of course, she caused the wreck!'

Tim took her by the arm. 'We'll back up and take another route to the hospital. This road will be blocked for a while until the wrecks are cleared away.'

She let him lead her from the unhappy scene and help her in his car. She sat in a grief-stricken daze as he manoeuvred the car around and then drove up a hilly side street which would take them to an alternate road to Biddeford.

Tim's face was white. 'Maybe it isn't all that bad! Their injuries may only be minor.'

'The trooper didn't seem to think that,' she said as Tim drove at a high speed along the back, wooded road.

They finally reached the outskirts of Biddeford. She knew the hospital was located on the main highway just inside the town limits and she watched the signs and directed Tim where to turn in.

They enquired at the lobby desk and were told to wait. No report had come down from the operating room yet, where the patients had been immediately taken. Now they began a vigil which was to last for a couple of hours.

Tim said, 'I'd better get in touch with Roger Deering and tell him. The party at the Colony may not have heard about the accident yet.'

'Yes, do that,' she agreed.

He went to the pay phone and put through the call. When he returned to her in the bleak light of the lobby, he looked very weary. He said, 'Roger and the others just got the news. He's coming over.'

It was about twenty minutes before Roger Deering strode dramatically into the lobby. They rose to join him as he asked, 'Have you heard how badly they were injured?'

'They're upstairs in the operating room now,' Tim said.

Roger shook his head. 'What a night! What a season!' And he went over to talk personally with the woman at the desk.

He came back after a little and told them, 'At least none of the four people in the other car had anything but minor injuries and shock. We'll have to wait to find out about Ruth and Buddy.'

It was about two o'clock in the morning when the elevator door opened and the two doctors who'd been looking after Ruth and Buddy emerged. Roger knew them both personally as they were regular patrons of the playhouse. He went over to get the news while Tim and Jennifer remained quietly behind him.

Jennifer heard the older of the two surgeons say, 'Miss Crane has a crushed chest and a multiple fracture of her left leg. She's going to be in hospital for some time but she'll make a complete recovery.'

Roger Deering nodded grimly. 'And the young man?'

The surgeon said, 'That's a problem.

He has severe back and head injuries. We've done what we can for him. It will take a few days to know just how critically he's been injured.'

'Should he be flown to Boston for added treatment?' Roger asked.

'I wouldn't advise moving him,' the surgeon said. 'We may think it advisable to have a specialist flown here. His brain is the delicate area. We're not sure whether there has been any serious damage. He's still unconscious.'

'You will keep me informed,' Roger Deering begged them.

'Depend on it,' the older of the two doctors assured him. Then they continued on their way.

Roger turned to them with despair on his pleasant face. 'You heard him!'

'Yes,' Jennifer said. 'I think you should get in touch with Buddy's father at once. He's the owner of the Phillips Hotel Chain and Buddy is an only son.'

'I'll do that,' Roger Deering said. And he left them to go to the phone booth.

Tim and Jennifer stood there disconsolately. Tim said, 'What a way to end the season!'

She shook her head despairingly. 'I shouldn't have sent Buddy with her!'

'You couldn't have known what was to happen,' the handsome leading man said. 'I blame myself for leaving you alone. I knew Ruth was in a nasty mood but I never expected she'd behave as she did.'

'It almost sounds as if Buddy might die,' she said, her voice trembling.

Tim placed a comforting arm around her. 'Don't!' he said.

They waited for a little longer and then Roger Deering returned from the phone booth. The theatre manager showed the strain he'd been under. He said, 'I wasn't able to talk directly to his father, but I was speaking with his stepmother. She'll try and locate her husband. He's in San Francisco seeing about buying a hotel out there. It will take a while to reach him and then for him to get here.'

'No more than a day,' Tim suggested.

Roger sighed. 'I don't know about you two, but I need some black coffee. In fact I need a lot of black coffee!'

They left the hospital and drove to a shabby, neon-lighted diner along the main highway which catered to all-night business. A group of truck drivers were congregated and talking noisily at one end of the dimly lit diner. They went down to a deserted area at the other end.

A burly man in white cap and a none-too-clean white shirt open at the neck advanced to serve them. 'What'll it be, folks?'

Roger Deering made a weary gesture. 'A pot of coffee!'

They sat on three stools with Jennifer on the middle stool. She said, 'I know I won't sleep tonight.'

'None of us are liable to,' Tim agreed.

The coffee came and Roger Deering waited until the had a few sips of it. Then he gave Jennifer a strange look.

He said, 'It seems to me that Ruth has accomplished for you the last thing she'd ever intend to do.'

She was startled. 'What?'

'She's put you in the female lead of 'Six Rooms With View' as her understudy,' the theatre owner said.

She gasped. 'I'd never thought of that part of it. I've been too concerned about them!'

Roger Deering said, 'Now it's time to begin thinking about the show. Happily Buddy wasn't a member of the cast. We can get along nicely without him. But it means you will have to go on in Ruth's place and Helen in yours.'

'I'm not sure I can do it!' she said in a panic at the thought.

'You must,' Roger said evenly. 'Isn't that so, Tim?'

'He's right, Jennifer,' Tim said. 'You can't give way to nerves at a time like this. We can't close the show.'

'You're well up in the lines, aren't you?' Roger asked.

'I was,' she said despairingly. 'Right

now I can't think of a single line.'

'We'll call rehearsals for the morning,' Roger went on briskly. He was rapidly recovering from the shock and regaining his usual business-like attitude.

'And I'll give Jennifer any extra coaching I can,' Tim suggested.

Roger Deering had second thoughts. 'Why don't we hold the rehearsal at one then? And you use the morning to polish her in the part.'

'That would help,' Tim agreed.

She looked forlornly from one to the other and said, 'How can you expect me to concentrate when I don't know whether Buddy is going to live or die?'

'You mustn't dwell on that. There's nothing you can do to help Buddy at the moment more than keeping the play going. There are many others at the playhouse depending on it for a livelihood,' Roger reminded her.

Both Tim and Roger kept pounding this hard fact and she knew they were right. It was her responsibility to go on in Ruth's part and do the best she could with it. Tim drove her back to the boarding house at three o'clock. He kissed her goodnight and let her out of the car, promising to meet her at the theatre at ten the following morning.

There was a light on in the vestibule and when she went inside she was surprised to discover that some of the apprentices were still up and waiting to hear the latest word from her. Helen, Sybil and Randy Scott were all standing around the refrigerator in the kitchen with glasses of milk.

Helen rushed forward to ask her, 'What is the word?'

'Ruth will be fine, but they're worried about Buddy,' she said forlornly. And she explained the details.

The stout Randy shook his head grimly. 'That Ruth has always been a nasty one. The people she ran into were leaving our show. So Helen and I were right on the scene.'

Helen gave her a knowing look. 'You and I will be going on then!'

'Yes,' she said. 'I've just returned from being with Roger Deering. And he expects us to take over.'

'Easy for me but hard for you. The lead is so long!' Helen said.

'Tim is meeting me at ten to work on the part,' she said. 'So we'd better get right to bed.'

Brunette Sybil asked, 'When can we expect more word on Buddy?'

'I imagine some time in the morning,' Jennifer told her. 'Roger has notified his family. They may have to fly a specialist in to operate on him.'

They all went up to bed and from sheer exhaustion slept a little while. But Jennifer woke before the others around eight o'clock and had breakfast by herself. Then she took the script of 'Six Rooms with View' and went over to the theatre to study it. No one had arrived yet except the caretaker, who was busy with his cleaning duties and did not disturb her.

By the time Tim arrived she'd gone over all the lines and felt she knew them. Before they began rehearsing they used the theatre office to call the Biddeford Hospital. The word was that Buddy was resting easier and Ruth was doing well. With this welcome news Tim began coaching her energetically.

They worked on the stage and, since many of the scenes were between them only, they were able to actually plan the way they would play them. Once again she was aware of Tim's coaching capabilities and felt regrets that he did not recognise his talents in this direction.

They paused after an hour or so and sat on the stage. There were no chairs as the scene was an empty apartment. Tim gave her a smile of encouragement. 'I like the way you're doing the part. It's very different from the attack Ruth had, but it's equally good.'

'I listened to her every night,' she said. 'And I couldn't see myself doing some of the scenes the way she did.'

'I think your way is as good.'

'I hope so,' she said with a sad smile.

'It's bad enough to be thrown into this so quickly. I can only hope that it turns out all right.'

'You haven't given a bad performance in anything yet. Why worry about this?'

They resumed rehearsing and Tim showed her how to play some of the trickier moments to the best advantage. They were still on stage when Roger Deering came down the middle aisle of the auditorium around twelve-thirty. He smiled up at them and said, 'I've been watching you from the rear of the theatre. I've liked everything I saw.'

'Thanks,' Jennifer said, coming up to the foot-lights. 'Is there any other word from the hospital?'

'Only that Buddy appears to be coming out of his coma,' Roger said. 'The doctors are more hopeful and his father is arriving here tonight.'

Tim asked, 'Hadn't Jennifer better have coffee and a snack before we begin the main rehearsal?'

'Yes,' Roger said. 'And try and get a

little rest as well.'

She left the theatre and went straight to her room and stretched out on the bed and slept for twenty minutes. She was wakened when Helen came in to check on her about rehearsal. Then she went down and had coffee with the red-haired girl, after which they hurried to the theatre.

Jennifer had seen movies in which the understudy took over from an ailing leading lady to become a great star. But she found the reality little like the screen versions. The gruelling work which went into hastily preparing for a long part had never been shown in films. And even if she were a hit in the play, not many people would have seen her. The performance surely wouldn't make her a star. But she did want to keep the company from closing and this was the thing which motivated her. She also would have to learn the leading female part for the season's final play. This was to be the 'Prisoner of

Second Avenue' and again her part would be lengthy.

The final rehearsal lasted most of the afternoon. Roger Deering was more patient than usual but he was also meticulous about the performance details. He would not let the show go on in a careless production. By the time they finished at five o'clock, everyone was weary.

Tim walked her back to the boarding house. 'You needn't worry about tonight,' he said. 'Your performance this afternoon was excellent.'

'I'm tired, but I do have more confidence,' she agreed.

'Roger is pleased,' he said. 'I could tell. The big thing now will be to make yourself familiar with the next play.'

'I'm glad it's the final one.'

'For once, I can say the same,' he agreed. 'Yet it is a sad time. The end of the season and the end of summer.'

She gave him a warm smile. 'Of just this summer.'

'True,' he agreed.

They parted at the door and she went up and waited until Helen had taken a shower, after which she took one. Then both she and Helen had short naps again. It was important to be in as rested a state as possible before the performance. She ate hardly any dinner and reported for the theatre early.

She had remained in her own dressing-room, which she and Helen shared. The red-haired girl's good nature and funny comments kept her from becoming too nervous. At eight o'clock she was all dressed and made-up. She only waited for the summons to places.

At this time she couldn't help but think of the quiet, friendly Buddy. He had lately always been the one to announce the rising of the curtain. His pleasant voice would not be heard in the theatre tonight. All because he had gone with Ruth at her request.

While the most recent word from the hospital had been better, she was still terribly worried about the young man.

Now she heard Ken Chadwick calling five minutes in Buddy's stead. She took a final look at herself in the mirror and then left her dressing-room for the stage.

Tim was out there waiting for her. They would soon be making their entrances. He came to her and raised one of her hands and kissed it on the back. 'To save your make-up and still wish you good luck,' the leading man said.

12

Talk of the accident had been the main topic of conversation in Kennebunkport and the surrounding area for the past twenty-four hours. So the audience in the theatre that night were well aware that Jennifer was substituting in the play's lead at short notice. Most of them also remembered her as the apprentice who had earlier played other parts. When she made her entrance there was a warm round of applause to let her know that they wished her well.

It was the extra bit of encouragement needed to make her offer a top performance. With Tim as her acting partner she played the part with verve and gaiety. The first act curtain brought hearty applause and plaudits from everyone backstage.

Roger Deering came back to tell her, 'You're doing beautifully. And by the way, a visitor just arrived.'

'Who?'

'Stephen Phillips, Buddy's father. He came here after he left the hospital. I've had a good talk with him.'

'What's the word on Buddy?'

'He's much better, but his back injuries were worse than the doctors thought at first. It may be months before he'll be able to get around normally.'

'As long as he recovers.'

'Mr Phillips claims the doctors say he will,' Roger Deering told her. 'He knows you were a close friend of Buddy's and he's asked to see you after the performance.'

'I'd enjoy meeting him,' she said. And with a wry smile she added, 'If I live through the second act!'

'You will!' Roger Deering assured her.

And so she did. When the play ended she took a curtain call on her own. As soon as the curtain fell on the last curtain call Tim took her in his arms and kissed her.

'I'm proud of you,' he said tenderly.

It was the finest tribute of all. 'Thank you, Tim,' she said in a soft voice, her eyes sparkling with happy tears.

Then others crowded around her and congratulated her. It was an evening of achievement and if Ruth Crane had any idea of what she'd brought about it was certain she must have felt miserable. Her bad actions had resulted in a triumph for Jennifer.

Jennifer had just finished changing into her street clothes when a knock came on her dressing-room door. She opened it to Roger Deering and another man of middle age who so resembled the pleasant-faced Buddy that she had no question that it must be his father.

Roger Deering introduced him. 'This is Stephen Phillips, Jennifer.'

Buddy's father took her hand and smiled. 'May I congratulate you on a charming performance,' he said.

'I wish I had never had to go on,' she told him. 'I've been so worried about Buddy.'

'He's badly hurt but he will recover,' Stephen Phillips said. 'And at the moment that's all I can ask.'

'All any of us can ask,' she agreed.

Buddy's father said, 'I understand there is a pleasant coffee shop not too far from here. I wondered if we might go there for a little. I'd like to chat with one of Buddy's friends.'

She thought of Tim. It was likely he'd planned to be with her on this triumphant night. But she felt she could explain to him. She also felt she owed Buddy's father some of her time since she still felt guilt about the accident.

She told Stephen Phillips, 'If you'll just wait here a moment I'll see if I can free myself from an engagement I'd made.'

'I don't want to interfere,' Stephen Phillips said.

'It's not all that important,' she assured him. 'I'll just be a moment.' And she hurried off to Tim's dressing-room at the other side of backstage.

Tim was just saying goodnight to the

old character man and he turned to see her. 'Hi,' he said. 'I was coming to pick you up.'

She gave him an embarrassed look. 'It's about that I've come to see you.'

'Oh?'

'Buddy's father is here and he wants to take me out somewhere,' she said. 'I think he's upset. I might be able to help him.'

The handsome leading man smiled. 'Of course. I understand. He'd be more at ease if there were no third parties. Don't give it a thought. I'll see you tomorrow.'

'You're sure you don't mind?' she worried.

He bent and kissed her on the forehead. 'Of course I don't. I'm fully in accord with what you're doing.'

She went back to join Stephen Phillips with a lighter heart. The millionaire hotel owner had an expensive rented car and she directed him to the coffee house where Helen and Randy were doing their comedy act.

They arrived in time to get a table down front for the show. Helen and Randy gave a great performance and when it was over she briefly introduced them to Buddy's father.

After Helen and Randy left them Buddy's father said, 'I think those two should continue to work together. Their act is excellent.'

'So do I,' she agreed.

'I have a friend in Boston looking for a kind of permanent act for his lounge,' Stephen Phillips went on. 'I'm going to send him information about those two.'

She smiled across the table at him. 'That would be very kind of you.'

'I'd consider it doing my friend a favour,' he said.

'Where is your head office, Mr Phillips?'

'New York,' he said. 'So I'll be able to fly back here in a few days and every so often to make sure Buddy is making proper progress.'

'Was he able to recognise you?'

'Just before I left to come to the

theatre,' Stephen Phillips said. 'The doctor seemed to think this a heartening sign.'

'I'm so relieved. The word was bad at first and I blamed myself for what happened to him.'

'You shouldn't do that,' the middle-aged man argued. His brow wrinkled and he sighed. 'You know I have plenty of things for which I could blame myself if I chose to. But I think that is a negative attitude. I have been too demanding of Phillip many times. I've tried to make him do what I wanted without any consideration for his feelings. I see how wrong I was now.'

'I'm sure you've tried to be a good parent.'

'I have. But I'm objective enough to know my shortcomings. I can be stubborn and unrelenting. I expected him to take over the direction of my dinner-theatres at the end of this season. He objected, saying he wouldn't have enough experience. I insisted that he would. It was never settled. Now this has happened and it is settled for us. He won't be able to take on any kind of work for months.'

'I'm so sorry,' she said.

'Maybe it worked out for the best,' the older Phillips said with a sigh. 'I think I would have been angry with him for what I felt was letting me down. This way we haven't had the direct conflict.'

She gave Buddy's father a troubled look. 'I must be truthful, Mr Phillips. Buddy talked to me about the situation. I think he was right and you were wrong.'

He looked at her rather sternly for a moment. Then he reached over and patted her hand. 'I admire you for being honest with me. And I'm glad to know Buddy has friends like you.'

'He very much wants to make good on his own,' she said. 'He feels that then he may be more valuable to you. And that is right.'

Stephen Phillips nodded. 'I can see it now.'

They spent another half-hour at the coffee house and then he drove her home. He promised to see her again when he returned and she assured him she would visit Buddy at the hospital every day.

Helen was waiting for her when she went upstairs. The red-haired girl was full of excitement at Jennifer being with Stephen Phillips. 'He owns all those theatres! Did he offer you a job?'

'No,' she smiled. 'But he's going to write to a friend of his in Boston to see if he can get you and Randy a job with a friend of his there. It sounds like a great opportunity.'

'I can't believe it!' Helen cried, and hugged her.

Now Jennifer was faced with days and nights of sheer drudgery. Playing in one play and getting the long part ready for the next. Tim spent extra hours coaching her and this helped. But it was still a huge task for her. She also kept her word and saw Buddy at the hospital every day. She even tried to visit Ruth

Crane, but the bad-tempered actress refused to see her.

Buddy was able to talk with her now and she told him how Ruth was behaving. The good-natured Buddy smiled and said, 'I wouldn't worry about it. I understand Roger has paid her and is looking after her hospital bills. She's going to be ready to leave the end of the week.'

'I don't imagine she'll remain in Kennebunkport,' Jennifer ventured.

'Not after all the scandal of her drunken driving,' Buddy said. 'The people in the other car are suing her insurance company.'

'She was to blame. And to blame for what happened to you.'

He managed a forlorn smile. 'I'll be all right as soon as I get out of this traction.'

'You don't have to hurry,' she told him. 'When is your father coming back?'

'He's leaving New York next Friday and he'll be here for the closing performance,' Buddy said, betraying the fact his mind was still only on the playhouse.

She laughed. 'He's coming to see you, not the play.'

'He may as well see it when he's here,' Buddy told her. 'And by the way, he likes you.'

'I'm glad.'

'So am I,' Buddy said wryly. 'You're about my first friend he's ever approved of.'

After the opening night of 'Prisoner of Second Avenue' Jennifer began to relax a little. There were no more plays to learn and they would be able to coast through the week to the end of the season. It was a good feeling.

But it was also a bad time. Despite the excellent response her performance and those of the others in the cast had received, it was the final play of the season. Business was only fair and the weather was becoming cool and rainy. The best of the Maine summer was over.

Then Roger Deering made his announcement to the press that, starting with the next season, the Kennebunkport Playhouse would be a package theatre, showing only travelling package plays. It was a let-down for nearly everyone, but they tried not to show their feelings. For Roger it was merely a fact of life that the playhouse could only continue profitably with packages, and he had no choice.

But he did call her in and tell her that he was going to proceed with Buddy's suggestion and have an apprentice group giving performances in the theatre on Sunday nights only. R. Dudley Moffet had agreed to become a member of the teaching staff and he was offering her the post of director.

Sitting behind his wide desk, Roger Deering offered her a questioning smile. 'Well, what do you say?'

'I don't know.'

'You are planning to teach this year, aren't you?'

'I'm not even sure of that,' she said.

'I'd hoped you'd accept my offer,' he told her. 'Anyway, I'll leave it open for a little. Why don't you feel interested?'

'I don't think it would be the same,' she said. 'And there is no place in this set-up for Tim Moore.'

'No,' he said with a sigh. 'I'm sorry. But there isn't.'

'I'll think about it,' she promised.

That afternoon when she visited Buddy at the hospital she told him about her conversation with Roger Deering. She said, 'I'm glad he's going along with your plan, but I don't think I want to be a part of it.'

'If I'm on my feet I'll be here,' he promised. 'Why are you not interested? Because of Tim?'

'I suppose so.'

Buddy studied her from his hospital pillow. 'You're still in love with him?'

'I care a lot for him.'

'Has he talked to you? Asked you to marry him?'

'No.'

'Then how do you know his feelings?' Buddy asked.

'He's told me dozens of times that he cares for me!'

'Buddy showed a twisted smile. 'And I care for you. But a lot of good it does me.'

She reached out and took his hands. 'We've always been the best of friends, Buddy. We always will be.'

'Yes,' he said wearily. 'That's where it ends. Just the best of friends. Can you blame me for wanting us to have more than that?'

Her cheeks crimsoned. She had that old feeling of being disloyal to Tim. She said, 'I'm sorry, Buddy. It's late. I have to go.'

As she reached the door he called out, 'Say hello to Tim for me. Tell him I wish him luck!'

She drove back to the yellow boarding house knowing a confusion of feelings. And she determined that before the week was out and the company broke up she must have some sort of understanding with Tim.

That night there was a throwback to the warmer weather of the early summer. It was very pleasant and after the show Tim invited her over to the Shawmut Inn for a goodnight snack. As they drove to the quaint summer hotel by the ocean, she said, 'How often have you visited the hospital, Tim?'

'A couple of times,' he said carelessly.

'Do you think that's enough?' she asked.

'I suppose not,' Tim admitted. 'But I know Buddy is getting better and you're there every day.'

'He's going to be in hospital and convalescing a very long while,' she reminded the handsome leading man. 'Time goes slow for him. He appreciates visits.'

At the wheel Tim showed a guilty expression as he kept his eyes on the road. 'Sorry,' he said. 'I'll make a point to see him once or twice before I leave.'

'Do!' she urged him.

'When is his father returning?'

'Tomorrow night. He'll be here for the closing performance,' she said.

'The end of an era,' Tim said heavily. It was the first time since the notice that he'd betrayed his feelings of sadness about the change in the theatre's policy.

'I know,' she said sympathetically. 'I can't believe that you won't be back here another year.'

'I've had a long run,' he said with a bitter smile. 'I suppose I should have known it would eventually end.'

'You'll find another company. You said that yourself!'

'I guess so,' he said as they pulled into the Shawmut parking lot. But he didn't sound too happy.

They entered the lobby of the Shawmut, which was fairly busy for the time of year. Fred Short was behind the desk and his alert eyes behind the hornrimmed glasses beamed on her. He came out to greet her.

'You're great in the play,' he said. And he smiled at Tim. 'You two make a great team. I'm sorry we can't look forward to seeing you back again next year.'

'It seems that isn't to be,' Tim said with an attempt at cheerful casualness.

'I'm sorry about the change,' Fred Short said. 'But Roger assures me it has to be that or close the playhouse.'

'None of us would want that,' Tim said. 'I shall always remember the place. I've had some of the best moments of my life here.'

Fred Short nodded sympathetically. 'I'll hope that you'll be back one day.'

'I hope so,' Tim said.

They went on into the lounge and found a table where they could look out and watch the moon on the ocean. They were served and after a little they went out to stand on the balcony and study the lovely view in the open.

At the railing, she said, 'Fred sounded really sorry that you wouldn't be coming back. I'm sure most people feel that way.'

Tim smiled down at her. 'That's

some satisfaction.'

She felt the moment had come. She asked, 'What about us?'

'Us?'

'Yes. You know how close we've been. That I love you. I don't want us to part. Let's leave here together!'

Tim took her in his arms and his eyes met hers. 'I'm glad you understand that I love you. I do.'

Her eyes filled with tears of joy. 'Oh, Tim!'

He kissed her and held her close. Then he said, 'Don't ever forget this moment. I won't.'

'I won't,' she said softly. 'So we will leave together.'

Tim released her a little so that he could solemnly look into her eyes. 'No,' he said. 'That would spoil it. The thing I love is that you're twenty-one! I don't want to spoil that!'

'I'm old enough to know what I want! I want to be with you!'

He ignored this as he said, 'Twenty-one! It's a magical and wonderful age!

You should live every moment of it to the full! Get every bit of enjoyment out of it!'

'Tim!' she reproached him. 'You said you loved me!'

'I love you as you are,' he said quietly. 'I wouldn't dream of making you different. That's why there can't be any future for us. I have nothing to offer you, neither youth nor security. Don't you realise that?'

She fought to regain her self-control and bitterly she said, 'I think I've made a fool of myself this summer!'

He seized her by the arms. 'Don't say that! Don't ever think it! And don't be bitter, Jenny, because it's an end of summer. There are other summers ahead. Many of them!'

'Yes,' she said. 'But no more summers for us.'

'I'm afraid not,' he said.

She turned away from him. After a little she said, 'I'd like to go home.'

Nothing was said between them on the drive. But when he halted the car before the door of the yellow boarding house and before he let her out, he leaned across and kissed her again and said, 'I want you to know it's been a wonderful summer for me, Jennifer. The most wonderful one of all my life!'

She threw the car door open and ran into the house and up to the bedroom. And she tried to stifle her sobbing as she prepared for bed so that she wouldn't waken Helen or Sybil. Before she slept her pillow was moist with tears.

Appropriately the last two days of the season were dull and cold. Somehow she got through them. Tim behaved kindly towards her when they were together backstage, but she thought he looked years older and careworn. They avoided any personal conversation.

Stephen Phillips returned for the weekend to see Buddy and attended the closing performance on Saturday night. She was grateful when the older man came backstage again and invited her to go to the Colony with him.

When they reached the lounge of the popular hotel it was only sparsely filled. Already the summer crowds were departing. He said, 'Buddy is doing very well. In a few weeks I'm having him sent down to our home in Palm Beach. He can convalesce there and the doctor says swimming therapy will be wonderful for him. By this time next year he ought to be healthy again.'

'I'm glad,' she said, wanting to be good company and feeling that she wasn't.

Stephen Phillips asked her, 'What about you?'

'I have a position teaching school dramatics near Boston,' she said.

'Excellent,' he said. 'Then you'll have a chance to see your friends Helen and Randy in the café there. They've been given a contract, you know.'

'They told me,' she said. 'I'm glad for them.' As she finished Sybil came in with the young man she was going to marry. They smiled and waved to her, then they sought a table of their own. She told Buddy's father about them.

He asked her, 'When are you leaving?'

'Monday morning,' she said. 'I don't need to hurry.'

'See Buddy before you go,' his father suggested. 'I have to leave tomorrow.'

'I mean to visit him,' she said with a smile. 'The last thing I do.'

It seemed there were nothing but farewells the next day. By the time Monday morning arrived and she was ready to drive back to Boston, after a stop to see Buddy on the way, she was the only one left at the yellow boarding house. She said goodbye to Mrs Thatcher and stepped outside with her bags in hand.

Roger Deering drove up in his sports coupe and poked his head out the window. 'Hello,' he said.

She turned from placing her bags in the trunk of her car. 'Hello,' she said wanly.

The producer's handsome face showed

a smile. 'You haven't told me whether you're coming back next year or not.'

She shrugged. 'If the offer is still open I'll take it.'

'Wonderful,' he said. 'I'll be writing you later when I have the plans more outlined. By the way, I've just seen Tim off. He asked me to say goodbye for him and wish you a happy year ahead.'

'Thanks,' she said in a small voice. 'That was nice of him.'

Roger gave her a knowing and somehow sympathetic look. He said, 'He'd have made it sound better than I did. He's quite a person!'

'Yes,' she said. 'Quite a person.' The pain was still there.

Roger drove away and she got in her own car and drove to the hospital. She found Buddy propped up by several pillows and in what seemed a good frame of mind. But then, he somehow always managed to be cheerful.

He said, 'So the season is over.'

'Yes,' she said. 'It's over.'

Buddy gave her a searching look.

'You do feel badly about it, don't you?'

Her eyes met his. 'Yes, I do.'

'Dad said he thought you felt badly. I'm sorry. What about Tim?'

'He's gone back to New York.'

'So has my father,' Buddy said. 'And one other thing. I've fixed up Dad with a director for his dinner-theatres. He had counted on me, you know, and he didn't want to keep the man he has now. So I told him the best man I knew for the job and he's going to see his agent right away.'

There was something in the way he said this which caught her interest. 'Who?' she asked, rather breathlessly.

'Tim Moore,' Buddy said, smiling. 'It's a top job which can really do things for him. And he's proven he's a good director.'

'Buddy!' she exclaimed happily, and she rather recklessly threw her arms around him and kissed him.

'Easy!' he laughed. 'I'm still in a cast.'

'I'm sorry,' she said. 'And it is mostly my fault.'

'I'm sort of glad it happened. Things have worked out. I plan to come to the playhouse next summer. What about you?'

She nodded happily. 'Yes. I'll be here!'

He smiled. 'I think we'll make a pretty good team.'

'I'm sure of it. Working with all the fresh young apprentices.'

He reached beneath his pillow. 'Since we're planning to be together next summer I'd like to make it sort of official. I asked my Dad to get me the largest diamond he could find in Biddeford. It isn't all that large, but I'd be happy if you'd accept it from me.'

'Buddy!' she exclaimed tenderly, staring at the huge diamond he was offering her.

'Well?' he asked. 'Is it a deal?'

She nodded and held out her finger for him to place the ring on it. Then they embraced for a long and meaning-ful moment. And she knew that while it might be the end of summer, it was the

start of something much more important. A new love and understanding
which would help her through all the
summers ahead!

THE END

We do hope that you have enjoyed reading this large print book.

Did you know that all of our titles are available for purchase?

We publish a wide range of high quality large print books including:
Romances, Mysteries, Classics
General Fiction
Non Fiction and Westerns

Special interest titles available in large print are:
The Little Oxford Dictionary
Music Book, Song Book
Hymn Book, Service Book

Also available from us courtesy of Oxford University Press:
Young Readers' Dictionary
(large print edition)
Young Readers' Thesaurus
(large print edition)

For further information or a free brochure, please contact us at:
Ulverscroft Large Print Books Ltd.,
The Green, Bradgate Road, Anstey,
Leicester, LE7 7FU, England.
Tel: (00 44) **0116 236 4325**
Fax: (00 44) **0116 234 0205**

Nina, anxious to save her marriage to Charles, wants to stop the rot before it's too late. Charles, refusing to admit that there is anything wrong, tells Nina to stop imagining problems. But there is her step-brother, Duncan Stevens — easy-going and artistic, everything that Charles is not . . . Charles' sister-in-law likens divorce to a mere game of chess — yet the effect of a tragic death, seven years previously, triggers off a happening of such magnitude that Nina faces the truth at last.

PASSPORT TO FEAR

Patricia Hutchinson

Rose and Ray, two young women travelling by ship from India to England are alike in appearance. Both orphans, Ray is wealthy, while Rose has lived on her wits. Ray has a heart condition and is going to England to her guardian. But then when she dies Rose takes on the other girl's identity. However, in England Rose becomes a victim of her new guardian's greed and her life is threatened. Can she yet find love and happiness?

SMILE OF A STRANGER

Mavis Thomas

When Ruth Stafford joins her mother at the Sea Winds Hotel, she has misgivings about Cecily Stafford's imminent marriage to Willard Enderby. Ruth suspects he has designs on her mother's recent legacy. If so, she is determined to unmask him! She is helped by another hotel guest, and finds herself falling deeply in love with him . . . but is this endearing stranger any more trustworthy than Willard? Joys, heartbreaks and divided loyalties lie ahead before her questions find answers.

CRANHAMS' CURIOS

Chrissie Loveday

After her hectic London life, Rachel returns to her native Cornwall and her parents' Curio shop. Things are changing and she realises that she is needed. There is plenty to do and the local vet, Charlie is an added incentive to extend her stay . . . but he has a serious girlfriend. Can she make a new life in St Truan or will she miss the city life? Will she stay for just a week or is it a lifetime commitment?

THE HEART'S RETURN

Dorothy Taylor

Painful memories surface when Megan Moore receives an urgent request from Jordan Alexander, at her agency Time Savers. Jordan, having purchased Megan's old family home, wants the property to be made ready for him to move in by the end of the month. Despite her knowing the work would prove an emotional minefield, Megan's interest in Jordan, and the chance of seeing her old home again, are both irresistible. Can she lay her memories to rest and find happiness again?